CAN'T BUY ME LOVE

When Jane Duncan's beloved grand-mother died, she left Jane the cottage in the little Scottish village where she had spent so many happy hours as a child. Relieved to leave the city life behind, Jane soon moved in. Her grandparents had lovingly tended the neighbouring Shaws estate as house-keeper and head gardener for many years. But Shaws has just been sold to Connor Macaulay, a wealthy Ameri-can businessman whose plans could mean the end of everything Jane holds dear. Sparks fly when they meet . . .

JO WEEKS

CAN'T BUY ME LOVE

Complete and Unabridged

LINFORD
Leicester

First published in Great Britain in 2016

First Linford Edition
published 2018

A catalogue record for this book is available
from the British Library.

ISBN 978–1–4448–3547–2

1

Sitting down on a cushion of moss against a sun-warmed rock, Jane stretched her legs out comfortably, basking in the sun's warmth. Her old dog, Pip, lay down beside her, turning round and round three times in the way he had done since he was a puppy, and Jane rested her hand on his side. 'It's good to be here, isn't it, Pip?' she said aloud.

It was so different from her poky little flat in Edinburgh. Her struggle to get to work every day on cramped buses, and the hectic, faceless work at the shipping office, seemed another world away. Inwardly she blessed her grandma once again — her dear, sweet grandma, whom she still missed so much. *Darling Grandma. Thank you for the cottage. I hope I can look after it well.*

Since leaving her city job a year ago, she had felt truly at home in a way that

Edinburgh could never be. 'And a good thing too, eh? You hated it,' she said to Pip, who wagged his tail in response.

Jane sighed. It was time to get on if she was going to do any more work in the garden today. Whistling to Pip, she got up, muscles protesting after the short rest, and took up her spade again. She kicked at a stone and smiled, watching it spin away. How many times had she longed to do that in London streets? And now there were no smart shoes, no bustling crowds, no deadlines to hurry to. She was her own boss, and she could kick stones in her own garden all she wanted.

Jane turned towards the cottage. Fiona, her cousin, was leaning out of an upstairs window, waving a pair of secateurs in her hand. 'Jane, are you finished yet? Do come in if you can. That phone call just now was Mrs Anderson. She told me that Shaws has been sold to a man called Connor Macaulay — and I want you to tell me all about him!'

Jane stared up at her. 'What did you just say?'

Fiona leaned even more precariously out of the window and nearly dropped the secateurs as she tried to reach a climbing rose. 'I seem to be about the only one in the village who's never met him, and Mrs Anderson said you both got on very well when you met last year.' She cut the rose and stretched out for another one. 'What I don't understand,' she said conversationally, 'is why someone should be so secretive about someone they've danced with so well — according to half the people I met this morning!'

Jane's stomach lurched. 'I'm sorry, Fiona — I'm standing here with my mouth opening and shutting like a goldfish!' She managed a smile. Shaws *sold*? To *Connor Macaulay*?

'And? You never told me you met him because . . . ?'

Jane took a deep breath. 'Oh, it wasn't anything really . . . just a misunderstanding that was a bit embarrassing . . . ' Her voice died away as the memory came back to her in clear detail.

* ★ ★ ★

It had happened last year, on one of Grandma's bad nights, and Jane had hardly slept. It was six o'clock by the time she'd stumbled downstairs to make herself tea and step outside for a breath of fresh air. She was overwhelmingly thankful that Grandma had at last been able to find peaceful sleep, but knew that the respite wouldn't last for long.

Outside it was very still. It was really too early for most people to be awake, and the dawn chorus had ended hours ago. She could hear the occasional squalls of herring gulls following the fishing boats going out to their work, but this only emphasised the quietness. She wandered here and there around the garden, her feet leaving marks in the dew; then on impulse she went through the wicket gate into the Shaws estate next door.

It was the first time that she'd opened the gate since her grandparents had retired from their work at Shaws thirteen years ago, at the end of the war. It always stood there as a reminder; there was not a day that passed when she did not think of the beautiful gardens and spacious, welcoming rooms of Shaws.

It was all just as she remembered it. There was the weeping willow where her kite had come down and stuck. There was the ancient yew, dark and hollow, under which she had had endless tea parties with her dolls and the little tea set given to her one Christmas. Here was the old oak side door that they'd always used, with the clematis a hazy pink around it.

A sea mist had sprung up, hiding the sun, and she was starting to feel increasingly chilled in the early-morning air. A few more moments of walking and she started to feel actively cold. *Well, what a surprise!* she chided herself. *Of all the silly things — to go out for a stroll in nothing but a nightie and a flimsy housecoat. What would Grandma say!* She stepped out briskly. Then she swung around the laurels and nearly cannoned into a complete stranger. They'd both stopped short, and stepped back; a second's difference and they would have collided.

Aware of her inadequate clothing, Jane experienced a moment of pure fear before adrenaline kicked in. Then she was angry enough to see off a dozen prowlers — even a prowler clad in an expensive greatcoat, using aftershave straight from heaven, and looking like a cross between Cary Grant and Gregory Peck.

'You're trespassing,' she said through gritted teeth. 'Get out of here. Now.'

* * *

Jane wrenched herself back into the present and tried to smile at Fiona, who was looking at her interestedly.

'Oh, I bumped into him wandering around in the grounds of Shaws early in the morning and thought he was a burglar. We had a bit of an argument, and he took himself off. And then there was a great rumpus in the village about the heir to the Macaulays turning up, but I didn't realise it was him . . . and I met him at the official welcoming do . . . '

'And you had to be polite to the burglar, though you were longing to tell him what you thought!' supplied Fiona, laughing. 'Oh well, at least if he's a businessman he's unlikely to be here very much.'

Jane agreed with her, trying to be nonchalant, and escaped Fiona's questions as soon as she could. She argued to herself that Fiona was right — new neighbours were always a worry, but surely everything would blow over. It *was* unlikely that the man would actually live in the place, after all. It had been empty for so long, it didn't even have electricity, and Connor Macaulay was a rich businessman from the States.

*　*　*

But the next morning, sitting at the window seat of her little bedroom to brush her hair, it was less easy for Jane to detach her mind from the news. The knowledge that Connor Macaulay was going to be their neighbour was — well, it just had too many implications even to start thinking about it. It was better just not even to try!

Having resolved not to think for a single moment more about him, Jane found her fists clenching in her lap. She remembered how she'd so looked forward to that welcoming party at the castle, and had dressed so carefully in her formal dancing dress, spending ages on the fall of the plaid and arranging her hair so carefully. What a waste of time, seeing that she'd never danced that evening after all. Meeting Connor Macaulay had put paid to that — she'd been home in a temper within the hour!

And that evening had started out so well. She'd imagined a slightly younger version of old Andrew Macaulay. In his fifties, salt-and-pepper hair, a very straight back. A military man, perhaps, or a doctor like his grandfather. She'd thought that if he wasn't too old and decrepit, he could dance. Grandma had already met him at church and had said what a handsome young man he was, but Jane hadn't taken that at all seriously, because Grandma invariably called any man she liked under sixty a handsome young man. If only she had believed Grandma! Then she would have made the connection between the man she'd sparred with on that early-morning walk round Shaws and this Macaulay visitor! But she'd not had time or energy to think about anybody, with Grandma as frail as she was. She'd been spending most of her weekends — and her money — on coming up to see her from Edinburgh, and she'd been in a state of continual exhaustion and worry.

Jane winced as she remembered how pleased Grandma had been that evening, so small and frail amongst the pillows.

'You look wonderful, darling,' she'd said. 'I'm so pleased you're going to meet Mr Macaulay. We had such an interesting talk; it was such a shame you weren't able to be there.'

'Never mind, Grandma. It'll be lovely to meet him tonight, and we can compare notes tomorrow.'

'Such a handsome young man, and so like his grandfather in so many ways. Have you your spare handkerchief?'

Jane had to smile, remembering that. And she had certainly needed that spare hanky by the end of the evening — with tears of pure rage!

She stared out of the window at a pair of seagulls squabbling, and sighed. It was impossible to stop thinking of that horrid evening once she'd started. At the castle she'd hardly had time to tell Mary, Mr Farquharson's youngest daughter and her friend from her earliest days, how beautifully she'd arranged the massed banks of flowers in every room, before Mr Farquharson himself had seen her and borne her off to introduce her to Mr Macaulay.

'We're having waltzes to start with,' he'd said, 'and then we'll be having the reels ... Oh, Mr Macaulay, may I introduce Miss Duncan? If you'll excuse me, I must just have a word with the band . . . '

And she was staring at the man she hoped she would never see again. The prowler who'd nearly knocked her over, the man she'd had such a row with, was looking down at her with a completely unreadable expression on his face. Jane's toes curled involuntarily at the memory.

'You? You can't possibly be — ' She'd broken off the sentence, aware of all the other people around them.

'The long-lost descendant of the Macaulays? Or perhaps you were about to say, 'You can't possibly be the burglar I managed to scare off.' Or, 'You can't possibly be the hero who saved me from hypothermia by lending me his coat to put over my nightie.''

'I was not just wearing my nightie!'

Bother the man — she'd only seen him for two minutes, and he'd managed to make her furious all over again!

Jane jumped up hurriedly and ran

downstairs. It was her turn to do the shopping, and she was not going to get angry remembering a year-old set-to with some upstart Yank!

★ ★ ★

Unfortunately, as soon as she'd started her trail round the little row of shops in the village, hampered by an increasingly heavy shopping basket and the good manners that forbade her to cut conversations short, Jane realised that her good resolution had one flaw. Everybody else was also thinking about the new owner of Shaws. They wanted to talk about him, too.

Did she not think he was handsome, now? (Mrs Stevens, at the grocer's).

Was she not pleased that that nice young man with links to the village — nay, a direct descendant of the Mr Macaulay whom her own dear grand-parents had known so well — had come back to his family home? (The minister, in Anderson's newsagents, with Mrs

Anderson joining in the conversation.)

Mr Macaulay was going to set up a bed and breakfast establishment. (Mr Howe, owner of the only bed and breakfast establishment in the village).

That American was already planning to tear everything down and build modern houses on the estate. (Murdo McLeod, who had been hoping that the National Trust for Scotland would buy Shaws).

And, of course, everybody wanted to ask tactfully about how Jane *felt* about Connor Macaulay moving into the house her grandparents had looked after for so long. Everybody was politely, but quite insatiably, curious about the matter.

By the time she got back to the cottage, Jane was ready to throttle the lot of them, and had decided that the only way to get back any peace of mind was to work in the garden for the afternoon. As she put away her shopping and made lunch, she thought grimly that it was lucky Fiona was out for the day, because she would have had to put up with an extremely bad-tempered housemate.

'You'll have to take the brunt of it, you know,' she warned Pip, who was lying down by the back door recovering from the exertions of the morning. She opened the door with some difficulty, stepping over Pip. Closing it behind her, she leaned back against it and stopped for a moment, just to look.

However many times she had entered the garden this way, the scene before her always made her catch her breath with its quiet beauty. The garden was so elegant and spacious with its soaring beech, sweep of lawn, and little orchard of fruit trees. The artist's studio was an airy white pagoda set amongst the bamboo. And meanwhile the cottage behind her, made of the same stone as the massive walls of the garden, was hardly noticeable, small and workaday, half-hidden with roses and climbing apple and pear espaliers.

Even using the paraffin flamer to get rid of the weeds on the gravel paths — a regular job, and usually a certain way to get rid of a bad temper — only partially managed to calm Jane down. She heard Fiona coming back but decided to stay out in the garden until she'd finished. Maybe she'd be in a better mood once she'd tired herself out with some heavier work.

Halfway through cutting back the bamboo patch, she admitted inwardly that she felt so angry partly because she felt so helpless about the whole matter. She could do nothing about Connor Macaulay owning the house next door. She could do nothing about how he might behave as a neighbour. Fiona and she — indeed, the whole village — were stuck with him!

Gathering up a bundle of long bamboo cuttings, she took it to a shady spot and, sitting down on the grass, started to strip the stalks so they could be used as canes. After she had finished the bundle, she stacked them neatly together and gathered up the leaves. Then she rested for a moment.

It was never completely silent in the

garden. Even in the quietest moments, the air was alive with birdsong and soft movements of the trees. Today the sounds seemed particularly beautiful as sunlight shimmered through the fresh leaves of early summer.

Jane found herself thinking about the man who had created this garden, as she often did when working in it. Dr Andrew Macaulay had planned it and planted it sixty years ago, knowing that he would not see its full maturity. Even if he had stayed on at Shaws, he would not have lived to see the beech tree grow to such a height in the corner, or that rambling rose covering so much of the cottage walls. He had been truly unselfish, planting for the enjoyment of those in the future, not an immediate show.

She thought that this garden showed the true nature of its maker. Andrew Macaulay had been a good man, a doctor whose care for others and devotion to duty was still a byword in the village. His hobby — his passion

— had been painting. The village had been an oasis in the desert for many artists after 1914. Many a shell-shocked young man had sought refuge in the translucent skies and perfect landscapes around Crail.

Dr Macaulay had cared for these poor lost souls, and encouraged them to start to paint again. He had built a beautiful artist's studio in his walled garden for his friends; he liked to paint in it himself, never thinking that his own daubs would ever be of any value. He had not realised that his unerring instinct for beauty and form would mean that even his shaky efforts would have value in the eyes of the art world, as the paintings of a great collector.

The artist's studio had been designed with care for its aesthetic appeal, but also with the most rigorous attention to detail and practicalities. The surveyor she'd had to look at the property had said it would probably stand for as long, if not longer, than the cottage, although the cottage had stone walls a metre thick and the studio was made of wood, a little gem of Art Deco architecture in its gentle Scottish setting.

And Dr Macaulay had been kindest of all to her grandparents, making over to them their servant's cottage, the studio, and the walled garden in which these buildings stood, when he sold the estate and left for Boston in 1921. Jane thought sadly that it was ironic that she had such strong good feelings about most of the Macaulay family — and just the opposite for the only one she'd ever met.

She got up and went over to the gate in the wall. Leaning over it, she looked at the beautiful sweep of lawns leading up to the old house. The shape of the original gardens was still clear despite their overgrown state, and she sighed as she remembered how beautifully her grandad had kept them. He hadn't been able to do much of the work himself by the time she was old enough to notice, but he had made sure that Jamie kept it as he would have done. Since Grandad's death, Jamie had been given less and less work to do in the garden. A big English firm had bought the estate ten years ago in 1947, with ideas of making it into a hotel. Outline planning permission had been granted, but in the end the firm had not gone ahead with the changes. Up to now the very minimum had been done to ensure its upkeep, and now the lad would probably be sacked altogether.

For a moment, Jane wondered if Connor Macaulay could possibly be persuaded to take Jamie back on full time, and then she told herself sternly that she must get used to the idea that the gardens — the whole estate — would soon look completely different. She had tried to persuade Murdo McLeod that his worries were groundless, but he was right. Next year it was quite possible that she would be looking at building work over this gate. She remembered the worry the English firm's plans had given her grandparents. She hadn't really understood at the time. Now it was her turn to worry.

Suddenly she became aware that Fiona was calling her, and was startled out of her reverie. 'Jane, there's someone at the door. Could you answer it, please? I've only just got out of the shower.'

The cool of the house made Jane realise how hot and dusty she was, and she pushed her hair back from her forehead with a grimy hand as she opened the door.

'Miss Duncan? I don't know if you remember me. We met last year . . . '

It can't be you. It can't!

2

Connor Macaulay smiled down at her with what she could have sworn was a twinkle in his hazel eyes. The sun lit up his hair and silhouetted his taut, lean frame. He had rolled up his shirtsleeves. The dark hair on his tanned forearms highlighted powerful muscles.

Even in the first moment of recognition, Jane was only too aware of what she had been trying to forget ever since she had last set eyes on the man — that he must be the most perfect specimen of manhood she'd ever come across in her twenty-six years. *I'm sizing him up as if he were some species of tree I was buying for my garden!*

She had last seen him at the official welcoming evening a year ago, in a beautifully cut suit — suave, diplomatic, a consummate international businessman. The time before that, at dawn in the grounds of Shaws, he had laughed at her, and she'd thought he was a scruffy holidaymaker. Now he was standing at her front door in dark trousers and a simple white cotton shirt, and he looked almost like a pirate! She was too stunned to do anything more than utter conventional words of welcome, aware that Fiona would be down at any minute and would expect no less. She found herself inviting him in . . . he must be tired after his journey . . .

'I'm afraid my grandma died just after you visited last year. But my cousin Fiona and her husband David are with me while they're looking for a house. I don't think you've met . . . David is in London at the moment, but Fiona is here . . . Please do stay and have some tea.'

'Why thank you, Miss Duncan. I'd be delighted to visit for a while. But I sure am sorry to hear about your grandma. She was a fine lady. I was honoured to meet her.'

He held his hand out — *just like an*

American in the movies! — and Jane took it. As they formally shook hands, the touch of him sent a shiver running down her spine. All her senses centred on his touch, and she could think of nothing but the warm, firm feel of his hand clasping hers.

With a start, she realised that he was looking with concern at a jagged cut on her hand. She realised she'd winced as he'd taken it, and not noticed.

'Your hand is hurt,' he said quietly.

The air seemed to be very still around them. She looked down at the bleeding gash on her thumb and suddenly realised how filthy she was from the garden work she'd been doing. Her hand looked small and grubby in his. She became aware of her ancient clothes, her grass-stained and earth-streaked knees where she'd been kneeling down, and the overwhelming smell of burnt paraffin that hung about anyone who had been using the flamer for longer than ten seconds.

She drew her hand back and found herself babbling, 'It's nothing, really; I just bashed my hand when I was gardening just now.' Looking up, she found his eyes fixed on her face, and could not look away.

Behind her, she suddenly became aware of Fiona coming down the stairs. The spell was broken. Jane was glad to turn away from him to introduce the two of them to each other, and escaped as quickly as she could to change her shirt, wash her hands and face, put a plaster on the cut, and drag a comb through her hair. As she did so, she thought detachedly that she had never really seen hands like his before. Tanned and strong, the fingers were surprisingly long and delicate. He had the fingers of a musician; she found herself wondering if he played the piano or the violin.

Coming back downstairs, she found them drinking tea in the living room. Fiona, born hostess that she was, had betrayed no surprise at Connor's presence. In fact, she invited him to supper as soon as Jane returned. Connor, with one slanting glance at Jane, accepted.

Jane was very thankful not to have to do any more than take a passive part in the conversation. Connor was asking Fiona about her painting, and Fiona was clearly happy to talk, which was unusual, as she normally disliked discussing her work with anybody except David, and showed very few people her paintings.

When Fiona offered to show Connor the studio, Jane excused herself and pottered in the kitchen. Her cousin had already made supper, a favourite Marguerite Patten stew, which had been in the oven for an hour already. Preparation was very quick, as all that was necessary was to set the table, put out a loaf of their homemade crusty bread and a new pat of butter, and mix a salad.

It was not long before she was able to curl up in her favourite chair next to the stove with a cup of coffee, Pip at her feet. She thought vaguely that perhaps she ought to go and be sociable, but felt terribly reluctant. She told herself that she was too tired, but that wasn't true; she had become excessively wide awake. She did not want to think why, but Connor's presence had hit her like a blow.

She told herself that in any case she should brush and feed Pip before doing anything else. She was darned if she was going to change for dinner. Fiona never did, but then Fiona always looked wonderful whatever she was wearing. With an artist's sublime confidence, she dressed and put on makeup extremely carefully, and then did not give her appearance another thought. Jane sighed and then told herself to relax.

She got up on hearing Connor and Fiona returning from the studio, talking about an exhibition of Peploe paintings they had both visited in Edinburgh. As she opened the back door to welcome them in, the fresh air came to her like a tonic. All at once aware of how lovely the evening was, she smiled at Connor.

Fiona, walking beside him, drew in her breath sharply. She was startled for a moment; she had never seen that particular expression on Jane's face before. Then she glanced at Connor. He had been smiling during their conversation, looking relaxed and humorous; but now there was a softer, almost luminous light in his eyes as they rested on Jane.

They're reflecting each other, she thought, *and neither of them realise it yet. I can't wait to tell David!*

Fiona liked Connor straight away. It wasn't surprising — that evening he was courteous, and a good companion, ready both to listen and to tell a story with that slow-spoken American accent that sounded so exotic and cosmopolitan in their sleepy corner of Scotland.

By the end of supper, Jane also felt so at ease with him that she showed him round the garden at his request. She ended up talking with him about it for almost an hour, wandering about, Fiona coming to join them, drinking coffee under the beech trees.

'It's just like my grandpa described

it,' said Connor. 'I remember him telling me about it when I was little — nobody else in the family was really interested.'

'Didn't you have any photos or paintings?' asked Fiona.

'Well, Grandpa did have some diaries and photos from Scotland, but my aunt burnt them with a whole lot of other papers when he died — my father was furious, because they were joint executors and she did it without telling him. There's a couple of sketches and paintings of the walled garden in the Macaulay collection, and some better ones in other museums, but none of them are great. They don't give any sense of what this place is really like.' He paused. 'It's magical.'

Jane looked at him with approval, but the gardener in her was forced to argue. 'I know at first glance everything might look beautiful and romantic, but it's sixty years since Doctor Macaulay designed it. It needs a complete overhaul. Almost all of the plants are original, and they're really old and tired.'

Connor looked at her in surprise. 'Well now, that's amazing. Didn't your grandparents change anything?'

'Well, no . . . they felt so loyal to the doctor, and were incredibly grateful to him for giving them the cottage and the studio and the garden. It was important to them to keep things just the way they had been. Like after Granddad died, everyone tried to get Grandma to grass over some of the vegetable plots and so on, to make less work, but she wouldn't.' Jane laughed ruefully. 'After I left school, I did a diploma in horticulture at the Edinburgh Botanies, so I kept on offering to help every time I came to stay, but by then Grandma hated anyone doing anything at all to the garden. She let me mow the lawn and weed, but that was it. She was sure someone would prune a tree so hard it would die, or secretly dig up half the herbaceous border. It's a shame, though, because it ended up with the garden in bad shape. Look — you can see lots of the trees and shrubs are overgrown. There's so little light under them. Even the woodland planting under these trees is all mossy and slimy.'

Connor's eyes were dark in the gathering twilight as he looked at her. 'So what are you planning to do with it now?'

Jane leaned forward unconsciously as she spoke. 'Well, I got term-time work in a school office near here last year, which is wonderful because up till then I was commuting to Edinburgh, and there was no time at all . . . I want to make the garden just as it was originally, using all the methods I've been trained in. And I'm hoping to develop a small business as a horticulturist, and designing gardens. So many of our gardens were completely changed with the dig for victory campaign . . . Some people want to get their gardens back to how they were originally set out, and others want all the new ideas . . . ' She paused.

'But there's another thing, too.' She paused again, wondering how best to explain it. 'When I lived in Edinburgh, I volunteered on a scheme helping disabled children to enjoy gardens and learn to be gardeners. That's how I got interested in gardening myself, actually. The school I'm going to be working at has a special unit for disabled children, and I'd like to try to set up the same thing here — no one's doing it in Fife yet. But I'll have to start by adapting the greenhouses, and that'll take a while.'

She stopped, surprised at herself. It was the first time that she had spoken about this idea to anyone. For a moment she felt embarrassed; then she didn't anymore, because Connor smiled at her, and she smiled back.

*   *   *

It was extremely late when Jane woke up the next morning. The quality of light filtering through the curtains warned her of what her clock confirmed — that she had slept for almost ten hours.

Lying in bed, thinking about the evening before, she owned to herself that the Connor she'd met last year seemed to have completely changed. *I can't believe it was really him! He's transformed — so polite and easy to get on with!* To be fair to him, though, she hoped he was thinking the same thing about her. Last year she had been so unpleasant to him. He might have laughed at her and dismissed her comments, but what else should she expect when she had been so aggressive herself?

After such an evening, it was even possible to think that Connor's furniture might be in quite good taste, and that he might not turn out to be such a bad neighbour after all. It was difficult to imagine somebody with the genuine interest he had in the history of their cottage, and his own family, razing the estate to the ground to put up new buildings, or filling the house with tubular steel monstrosities. In fact, she could almost say that she was looking forward to his moving into Shaws!

Jane was interrupted in these pleasant thoughts by the telephone. She rolled over and burrowed further under the sheets and blankets, hoping Fiona would deal with it. After a few seconds, the ringing stopped and Jane relaxed; but a minute later, Fiona called up from the foot of the stairs. Reaching out for her dressing gown, Jane stumbled down to the kitchen.

Fiona was there, looking horribly efficient and awake, brandishing the telephone receiver at her. 'It's Connor,' she announced with a bright smile.

Jane was still too dazed with sleep to demur. She took the phone.

'Jane, is that you?' His voice sounded strangely hesitant.

'Yes, it's me,' said Jane, and paused unhelpfully. It was beyond her to make polite conversation on the telephone five minutes after waking up.

'I was wondering if you'd like to get together some time in the next couple of days. Perhaps dinner? There's something I'd like to discuss. I've heard there's a restaurant called Rusacks in St Andrews that's quite good.'

Jane laughed — she couldn't help it; suddenly the morning seemed much brighter. 'Invite me to Rusacks and you can discuss whatever you like!' She put the phone down and turned to Fiona.

'Let me guess,' said Fiona, laughing. 'He's invited you out.'

Jane flung out her hands. 'I can't believe it!' She felt as if she could walk on air. Suddenly the whole room was full of electricity; she hardly dared to touch anything in case it gave off sparks. 'He just seemed so — so *nice* yesterday . . .' She trailed off; it was impossible to put how she felt into words!

★ ★ ★

Jane spent a good deal of the next two days trying to decide what to wear. Connor had not only invited her out to dinner at her favourite restaurant, but had also asked her if she would like to take a walk first around St Andrews itself, the little town in which it stood. She had accepted with pleasure. She knew the town well, and an evening walk there was breathtakingly beautiful at this time of year. Much bigger than Crail, it had several beautiful old buildings, as well as a castle and the old golf course that the restaurant overlooked.

Unfortunately, its quaint historical nature also meant that it had cobbled streets. Practically, Jane was aware that it was extremely difficult to do any walking there in anything but sensible shoes and very sensible clothes; she'd warned Connor. She would need her very old but dependable full-length oilcloth coat with her walking boots on this stroll. But how on earth could she combine an attractive outfit for one of the best restaurants in Scotland with the need to be comfortable and casual beforehand? If she wore high heels, she would end up hobbling, if not falling flat on her face. She thought wryly that she'd had enough trouble already being unsuitably dressed around Connor!

She went through her wardrobe a couple of times and discussed the whole thing with Fiona so much that even that paragon of virtue was starting to get a little frayed around the edges, and teased her that she was acting like a schoolgirl on her first date. Jane was indignant, and denied it fiercely. Fiona laughed and apologised, but Jane was uncomfortably aware that perhaps she wasn't convinced. For herself, she found it hard to pin down why she felt so pleased about Connor's invitation, or so nervous about what to wear. She argued inwardly that it was simple. Of course, that misunderstanding last year had taken on significance because of the unusual circumstances, and it was wonderful that it had all been cleared up. And of course she was relieved, because after all her worry, it looked as if their new neighbour would be quite nice after all, and it would probably be easy to get along with him.

As she thought this, Jane realised that she could still remember her hand in his; the stroke of his glance over the cut at the base of her thumb; and how their eyes had seemed to lock together. She had an odd fluttering feeling in her stomach when she thought about meeting Connor again.

In the end, she went to Edinburgh and spent far too much money in a little shop off Princes Street on a deceptively simple silky tunic and beautifully cut black trousers. She would be warm and comfortable in these with a fisherman's sweater and her long coat during the walk, and she could wear her walking boots and thick socks. When they got to the restaurant, she could change into thin sandals and take the sweater off to transform the outfit into a suitably elegant ensemble for the occasion. She was very thankful that they were going to a restaurant where the proprietors were locals born and bred. They were used to the diners doing this sort of thing, and had designed their cloakrooms accordingly!

On the day of the date, she gave up in the garden after making several mistakes, including weeding up some perfectly respectable seedlings in the vegetable border, and took Pip for a walk in the woods. She felt full of restless energy, but the exercise didn't calm her at all. On the contrary, the bright sunshine and the wind in her hair only served to make her feel rather light-headed. *I'm not going to think too much about this evening, or it will make me nervous.* She was very glad to have Pip along, who distracted her by periodically disappearing so that she had to call him back. *Perhaps I ought to think of some harmless topics of conversation. There's nothing worse than long awkward silences on a date.*

By the end of the walk, she'd decided to give up trying to think of witty anecdotes. She would concentrate instead on being a good listener, the sort of person who seemed genuinely interested in what another person had to say. *That won't be difficult when it's Connor Macaulay you're listening to, will it?* She resolutely put such thoughts away and hurried back to the cottage. She was going to be late.

Leaving Pip with a fresh bowl of water

in the kitchen, she dashed through a shower and left her hair to dry naturally as she pulled on the tunic and trousers. So much for the quiet understated look, she thought ruefully as she surveyed herself in the mirror. At least her lipstick didn't clash with the tunic. But she looked hot and bothered, her hair was wild, and her eyes seemed anxious. She ran downstairs and put her bag, sweater and coat in the porch, and checked her hair and makeup again.

Once she'd done it all, in far too much of a rush, she found she'd at least twenty minutes before she had to go. She had arranged to meet Connor at St Andrews Cathedral. Meanwhile, Fiona had gone down to Edinburgh for the day. Jane wished she hadn't. She would have liked someone to tell her she looked sophisticated and self-confident. At this point, her sense of humour got the better of her. *You're being so over the top it's just silly!* She chuckled aloud, felt a good deal less tense, and wandered into the studio, resolutely ignoring Pip's barks from the kitchen.

In the studio she stopped, struck by the work left casually on the easel. The painting, a landscape, was only in its early stages, with blocks of colour massed in, but it was quite a departure from Fiona's usual style of dreamy water-colours. Bold and uncompromising, it commanded her attention in a way that Fiona's previous work had not. Although Jane did not know a great deal about art, she guessed that it presaged a major development in her cousin's career.

Not for the first time, Jane felt a twinge of envy towards Fiona. Ever since her cousin's first exhibition in Cambridge, after her fine art degree there, her paintings had sold well. Continuing interest now ensured a steady income from art buyers and private collectors. Meanwhile, her ambition was taking a lot longer to achieve. She had financed her qualification at the Edinburgh Botanies with part-time work over four years, most of which had been office-based rather than horti-cultural.

Then she gave herself a little mental shake. After all, it had taken Fiona enough hard work to get to this point! She glanced at her watch. Bother! Now she was going to have to hurry!

She rushed out of the house and set off for the train station. Luckily there were very few people at the ticket office, and she was able to buy her ticket in plenty of time. Arriving outside the cathedral grounds, she breathed a sigh of relief. She had been sure that Connor would have started to drive back to Edinburgh after waiting for ten minutes, but she could see him walking through the ruins, a tall dark figure looking up at the delicate tracery of the remains of the chapel windows and shading his eyes against the sun. Going through the entrance gate, she went to join him, silently thanking her lucky stars that she had decided on her oilcloth coat, as the wind from the sea was cold despite the bright sunshine. She was glad to see that he, too, was casually but warmly dressed.

Then she caught her breath, and forgot clothes etiquette, as he turned to look at her. She could have sworn his eyes lit up as soon as he recognised her.

'It's good to see you again,' was all he said as they met, but he smiled. Then somehow, suddenly, she had drawn closer to him, and her heart was beating so loudly, so insistently, that she could think of nothing else.

3

'How's your hand now?'

'Oh, much better, thanks — see, it's nearly healed.' Jane put her hand out as she spoke, and he looked down. It was only a moment before there was a sharp fluttering of wings as a rook flew down onto the grass near them, and the spell was broken. But in that second, it was as if they were the only people in the world. The blue sky, the deep shadows on the grass, the myriad little creatures around them, the whole of creation suspended for one shimmering moment, and Jane thought breathlessly, *This is crazy! Why does the man make me feel this way? I hardly know him!*

She pulled herself together, jammed her hands back into her pockets, and said firmly, 'Shall we go along the West Sands first? It's a beautiful walk, there's an estuary you can see from the headland,

and we won't be able to go later because the tide's coming in.' She took a deep breath and added, 'I ought to warn you that although I can walk an awfully long way, I can't walk very fast.'

He looked down at her, tall and broad-shouldered, and smiled. 'Hey, tall guys can walk slow too,' he said. 'We have to, often, or we get to tripping over things.' And they set off amicably, Connor shortening the stride of his long legs to accommodate her pace. Jane noticed, and was inexpressibly gratified. She had a slight limp that only became apparent after a mile or so of walking too fast, from a badly broken ankle when she was a child. Although she could hike for hours, she could only go slowly, and was extremely self-conscious about it. Connor was the first male walking companion she had met who was perfectly courteous about it. Most men either walked ahead and then waited for her to catch up, saying it was impossible for them to alter their pace, or fussed, trying to take her arm or suggesting they walk even slower, after dragging every last detail about the accident from her.

Chatting, joking, they walked right up to the headland. The walk seemed to take only minutes. Connor had a way of listening that made her feel as if what she said was of immense importance to him; and he could make her laugh.

When they reached the headland, Jane was able to point out the estuary to him. They even thought they could make out a few seals on sandbanks in the distance, tiny grey blobs. 'More like slugs, really,' said Connor. Jane opened her mouth to protest and then saw he was teasing her, smiling down at her with the corner of his mouth quirked upwards in a way she felt she had known for years. Standing there with the sun in their eyes, wind whipping about them, driving his hair into a tousled mass and hers into a mane, she wished they did not have to go back to the restaurant so soon. However, the tide was already creeping up towards them.

'Seems a shame not to get to see them closer today,' said Connor, echoing her thoughts uncannily, as presently they turned with unspoken consent back along the beach.

For a while they were quiet, the only sounds the distant talk of the few other people on the beach, the rustling of the wind over the sand, the breaking waves, and the cries of seagulls overhead. It was a companionable silence, and Jane started to feel very happy. It was such a beautiful day. She stole a glance at her companion. He was looking sad and rather stern, in contrast to his relaxed, smiling demeanour only a short while ago. Suddenly Jane remembered that he had originally said he wanted to ask her something, and felt quite suddenly that she must — absolutely must — find out what it was. Now might be a good moment, while they still had time to talk in private, before they reached the restaurant.

'By the way', she said casually, 'what is it that you want to discuss with me?'

As soon as she had spoken, she

realised that her intuition had been correct. He turned and smiled at her, and said, 'You guessed what I was thinking about!' Then he hesitated, and said, 'I'd rather save the discussion I mentioned until later, when we can sit down over our meal and talk about it properly?'

'You sound rather worried about it,' Jane said carefully.

He smiled back, but his eyes still looked worried. 'The fact of it is, you might think it rude . . . '

Rude? This must be an Americanism. Or are we back with our grandparents in the Twenties here?

' . . . but I feel it's a couple of questions worth asking. Ten to one you'll say no, but it's just possible you might say yes, or . . . ' He paused.

Or I might say, 'Why, Mr Macaulay, whatever made you think I was that sort of girl? Do you think I have no one to protect me?'

Jane shook her head to get rid of the images flowering in her imagination.

'Well, now you've said all that, I can't bear the suspense,' she said cheerfully. 'Just bear in mind — it'll be an uncomfortable dinner if you're about to mortally insult me!'

She glanced at him, but he did not look reassured. There was an uncomfortable silence between them, and Jane frowned. The atmosphere had been so different only a moment before.

But to her pleasure, within a few moments he had recovered himself and managed to set the conversation going again. She felt quite unreasonably pleased. It was so civilised to be talking to a man who did not sulk. Rory had sulked dreadfully, and she had vowed never to go out with a moody person again. Dismissing one of her unsavoury adolescent love affairs — and several of her male acquaintances — with an inward smile, she looked at Connor with increased approval.

★ ★ ★

The restaurant — and her outfit — were all she hoped they would be. The look on Connor's face as she joined him for their meal — her hair brushed, makeup adjusted suitably, and high strappy sandals on — made her feel very pleased that she'd taken so much time and trouble. She took a deep breath and hoped she would remember to sit up straight and appear graceful and witty.

It was dessert before he got around to the subject she was waiting for. Evidently whatever he had to ask her didn't go with lemon sole or navarin of lamb. It wasn't until they were both toying with a particularly delicious soufflé — which they both agreed it was a shame they didn't really have room for — that Connor's expression took on that same rather sad, stern look, the conversation faltered, and he dropped his napkin.

Jane sighed. 'Spit it out, then,' she said trenchantly.

Connor looked at her in surprise. 'How did you know?' He stopped.

For a man of the world, she thought, he was certainly unsure about whatever he was going to say. His poise, his sure way with words, had left him.

'It's two questions. The first is — and please hear me out — I'd like you to consider an offer for your property . . . '

Jane sat very still, arms folded, her face set in stone. *He wants to buy my cottage!* She stared at him as he went on talking, swept away on a wave of contempt for him — yes, and for herself.

' . . . I would be prepared to pay twice its market value, or the value of any other property that came up for sale, if you wanted to stay in the village . . . You see, the reason I came back was to restore my grandfather's estate, and in some ways, your property is the most important part of Shaws. He told me it was the walled garden, and the studio, he loved best of all.' He paused and looked at her, and went on in his slow, careful voice. 'Please don't say no straight away. Give yourself time to think about it. Even if you don't want to sell now, the offer will always be open. Just let me know if you're ever interested in talking this through?'

Jane had not heard a thing since those first few searing words. When she had made that flippant remark about an uncomfortable evening, and mortally insulting her, she had not thought she was prophesying; she had meant it as a joke. It was impossible. Jostling images ran through her head.

Her grandfather falling from the roof of Shaws, trying to inspect storm damage, and insisting it was a job he had had to do. (*So this is how my grandparents' loyalty and hard work have been repaid!*)

Fiona's jokes about dreadful neighbours at Shaws. (*And this is the neighbour we have ended up with!*)

Herself, eagerly talking to Connor, showing him the cottage, blossoming under his interest in her plans for the garden. (*And all the time he was planning to annexe it, and as like as not build on it!*)

The bank statement she'd received that morning, showing that the clothes and shoes she'd bought for this date had very nearly emptied her account. *(And haven't I been a fool!)*

The silence between them lengthened, and Jane realised he had finished speaking. Well, she thought, she had better get it over with, and then they could both go home, and she would go to bed, and hope she woke up on the Riviera on holiday to realise that this was all a bad dream.

'No,' she said baldly. She saw him about to speak again, and said quietly, 'It's a shame that you didn't realise, when I was talking with you the other evening, just how much the cottage and the garden and the family connection to Shaws mean to me. I don't think you would've asked me if you had. The answer is no, and always will be no.' With an enormous effort she smiled and added, 'I hope that this won't affect our position as courteous and reasonable neighbours, but I'm sure you'll understand if under the circumstances I'd rather go straight back home now.' She gathered up her napkin and started to rise from her chair.

'Jane, please don't go.'

In the same moment he had half-risen too, and stretched out his hand to her. They were both breathing rather fast. He was looking at her earnestly, the pupils of his eyes wide and dark in the muted light of the alcove where they were sitting. Reluctantly, she sat down again, and he did too.

'I sure am sorry that I asked you to consider selling your house,' he said. 'I know you don't want to discuss anything to do with it, or any ways around it, and I won't mention it again. But I do want you to understand that it was something I just had to ask. There was the smallest of possibilities that you might've accepted the offer because of the capital it would've given you for setting up your business, for instance. No — ' She was about to protest again. 'I won't ask you again. I promise.'

Jane stared at him. She was aware of something lost, of a sense of desolation, as he looked at her. She remembered how just a few hours ago they had laughed together looking at the seals, his dark hair whipped by the wind, the sand blowing relentlessly around them. She shrugged her shoulders. 'Just so,' she said bleakly.

'You've forgotten I had two questions to ask you,' he said, looking at her seriously. 'I have to be away a lot over the next three months, and I need someone to oversee the changes I want to make to Shaws; to keep an eye on the builders and decorators, and let me know if there are any problems.' He named an astronomical fee, and added, 'Of course it shouldn't take more than an hour in all each day, but it does need someone prepared to go in and out. You might be able to fit it in with gardening, and it'd be over before you start your new job.' Without waiting for an answer, he smiled at her. 'I'd really appreciate it if you could let me know in the next couple of days, when you've had time to think about it. But why don't we just put the whole thing aside for now and enjoy the rest of the evening? Would you like some coffee?'

Jane was unable to do more than assent in what she hoped was a dignified way. She was uncomfortably aware that her jaw had dropped open at the offer he'd made, not to mention the amount of money he'd mentioned, and she was feeling quite dazed. But Connor didn't seem to have noticed. He signalled to the waitress.

In a few moments, Jane was actually drinking coffee with this extraordinary man. She was also detachedly aware that they were chatting again about the London theatre. *This man is driving me crazy!*

Their coffee finished, he asked her — rather diffidently, she thought — whether she would like to walk around the castle, as it would still be light for another half hour or so. *No way! You must be joking!*

'Yes, that would be marvellous,' she

heard herself saying — this poised figure that she did not recognise at all and who was smiling up at Connor in far too friendly a way.

She was uncharacteristically silent as they set out together towards the ruins of the castle, which were starting to take on a stark, eerie character in the evening shadows. Her mind was reeling. She was just beginning to recognise the implications of what he had said.

She could see why he wanted her property. Aesthetically, the walled garden and the studio belonged to the old house. So far, so good. He had asked her to forget he wanted to buy it, that his offer had been 'worth a try', but that he would not pester her over it. Not so good.

Could she trust him? No way! When he was so pleasant yesterday, and she enjoyed showing him the cottage, little did she know he wanted it for himself! With a cold feeling in her heart, she knew that from now on, whatever he said, she would always suspect him in his dealings with her.

And now he had asked her to oversee the conversion of Shaws! She did not understand at all. The very thought of what conversion he might be planning made her feel uneasy, although it couldn't be denied that the money would be extremely useful as an investment in her business. But did she want to become his employee, and dependent on his money? Could she trust him?

She thought gloomily that he probably had a hidden motive in offering her the job too, and started to walk at a pace that she knew would have its revenge on her ankle the next day. She could not believe that she had managed to speak so reasonably and politely in the restaurant. For two pins, now, she could hit him.

His long strides kept him effortlessly by her side, but she could feel herself starting to breathe fast. Speeding up even more, her foot turned on a rock, and the treacherous ankle gave way. With a cry of pain, she sank down onto the grass.

Within a moment he was kneeling beside her, solicitous, asking what he could do to help. Her exasperation finally gave voice and she snapped back: 'For goodness' sake! You could start by giving me a bit of space!'

He moved back hastily.

'First you insinuate yourself into my house, then you try to buy it from me, and now you've grounded me into the bargain!' She folded her arms and turned to look away from him. 'Just leave me alone and go away!' She paused for breath and tried hard to think of the most cutting thing that she could say. 'Snake in the grass!'

'Er — would that be a rattlesnake, now, or a cobra?'

Despite herself, her lips twitched. She stole a glance at him and saw him looking at her perfectly seriously and concernedly. Suddenly the humour of the situation hit her and she broke into laughter. She pulled her hanky out of her pocket and blew her nose defiantly. 'Don't you laugh — it isn't in the least bit funny. How can I go back home and live in peace with a boa constrictor next door waiting to swallow up my house any moment?'

She gingerly put her foot to the ground and grimaced as pain shot through her ankle. It was certainly a bad sprain this time.

'The thing is, if I slither away from here you'll probably have to roll back to the station,' he said. 'I don't see you walking on that foot right now without support. If I promise never ever to mention buying your house again, may I help you? Can I call a taxi for you, or drive you home? My car is parked nearby.'

She looked at him with all the pointed dislike that she could muster. 'I'd rather sit here till the ruins fall down on me. But then that would suit your purposes, wouldn't it? You'd be making an offer to my executors before I was cold in my grave!'

'Not at all,' he said equably. 'I'd have to wait for seven years to buy if you were under a pile of rubble and we didn't know what had happened to you, since I'd have run away — or more likely I'd go to jail, as everyone would decide I'd done away with you to suit my evil plans!'

Without meaning to, she glanced quickly at the looming ruined walls and shivered. He caught the look and knelt down beside her. 'Don't try to put your weight on your foot yet,' he advised her matter-of-factly. The next moment was a swirl of pain as he gently helped her upright. Jane still had her eyes tightly closed and her teeth clenched as they started to walk back. She heard the steady tread of his feet over the uneven ground and felt his arm around her, reassuring, warm. She stared away from him resolutely, trying to ignore the fact that he was so near. By the time they got back to the station, her ankle was feeling a good deal worse. It was all she could do to thank him formally.

'I'm so sorry, Jane. Is there anything I can do?'

She ignored his offers. 'Don't say sorry. It's not your fault I stumbled.' *Though actually it was your fault, because if it weren't for you I wouldn't have been walking so fast to get away!*

In the train, her innate good manners obliged her to lower the window for the final politenesses, however difficult it might be to say them. He leaned down, his height magnified by the position he had to assume. He looked worried, his brow furrowed as he held on to the door.

'You're sure you'll be OK?'

I very much doubt it after this evening! 'Yes, I'll be fine, thank you.'

'You'll let me know about the job, keeping an eye on Shaws?'

Like I would ever want that! 'I'll let you know.'

But instead of walking away, he continued to look at her, frowning. 'Are you really sure you are all right with that ankle? Perhaps I could drive you to a doctor.'

'Perfectly sure, thank you,' replied

Jane frostily. But he still stood there, gazing at her worriedly. As the whistle sounded and the train started to move, she relented.

'Look, Connor, I'll be fine. Believe me, this has happened lots of times. Your offers are very kind, but I'll be perfectly all right.'

He was still looking at her as the train drew away.

4

Over breakfast the next day, Fiona and David were incredulous. 'Tell me again — how much, exactly, did he offer you for the cottage?' gasped Fiona.

Jane shrugged her shoulders, feeling ruffled. 'I told you already. Twice the market price, or any other property which comes up for sale in the village.' She thought they would have been horrified at her tale of yesterday's disasters, and Connor's duplicity and underhandedness, but they didn't seem to be the least bit bothered by anything but this.

David got up, stroking Fiona's hair as he passed. 'Anyone else for more coffee? I need about six cups to get over the shock of hearing you turn down that sort of money.'

'You know I don't need it,' said Jane defensively. 'Especially from such an arrogant, selfish swine.'

A barely perceptible glance passed between Fiona and David. Jane was only too aware of it. She sighed. 'All right, I admit it. It's wounded pride. I thought he was interested in me as a person, and it turns out he's interested in me as the owner of a property he wants — and as a potential employee!' She gestured in frustration around her, the sweep of her arm including the whole of the patio area where they were sitting — the wicker chairs, the pergola, and the birds splashing in the birdbath nearby. 'For goodness' sake, we've got to put up with him as a neighbour knowing he wants to buy the place!' She practically spat out the words, and jumped up from the recliner, unable to stay still a moment longer. 'I'll help you with the coffee, David. I need something to do or I'll end up hitting something!'

She was still seething as they all walked up the path together to the back porch; but, pulling herself together, Jane asked David about how his work had been going over the last few weeks; she did not want to spend all morning hogging the conversation.

Fiona started to wash dirty breakfast dishes, and Jane automatically took up a tea towel to dry them. They talked about David's work, and it was not until he was filling the kettle and Jane was setting the mugs on the tray that he finished an anecdote about one of his colleagues and a little silence fell. He leaned back against the table and folded his arms.

'You're really worried about what happened yesterday, aren't you?' he said to Jane gently. 'But it seems to me Connor Macaulay's actually been very honest with you all the way along. Is there something else that's concerning you about him?'

Jane opened a drawer and got out the coffee spoons. She paused and thought, and then turned to David. 'It's true that he's been upfront about wanting to buy the house, but I know so little about him. It feels very odd that I've told him so much about myself and he's used that information — like the fact I'm hoping to start up a business — to try to manipulate me.' She opened the fridge and got out the milk. 'And meanwhile, I know he's a businessman — something to do with the Macaulay Art Foundation, and the grandson of Doctor Macaulay, and that's it.'

She poured the milk into a jug and set it onto the tray, rather more forcefully than she meant to. The milk spilt, and she hurried over to the sink to get a cloth, flinging the next words over her shoulder. 'I did a search in the library but didn't find out much more — the encyclopaedia has information on the foundation, but it has a low profile; it doesn't go for publicity. The only piece I found on him said that he never gives interviews.'

David stopped spooning coffee into the pot and regarded her thoughtfully. 'You know, I could probably find out more about him than that. A friend of mine from college is a journalist and did some research on private art foundations for an article in January. I could give him a buzz and ask if he knows anything.' He paused. 'Does he seem a particularly secretive person to either of you? It's strange he didn't tell you anything about himself at all.'

Jane tried to think back on their conversations and frowned. 'He's the sort of person who ought to be in the diplomatic service. He has a knack of sounding extremely interested in whatever anybody has to say, and asking the right sort of questions, so I ended up telling him all about myself when he came here. I didn't like to ask him about why he'd bought Shaws at first, because I thought it would sound as if we were nosy neighbours, and then . . . we just talked about other things . . . ' Her voice trailed off as she remembered the inconsequential, joking conversations they'd had.

Fiona turned to her. 'Well, he did tell us about his memories of Doctor Macaulay, how he didn't realise what the walled garden would be like, and how his aunt had burnt the letters and photos his grandpa had left. I got the impression he wasn't deliberately holding back on information, at least.'

Jane nodded. 'Yes, that's true. It's odd, isn't it, that the collection doesn't have many pictures of the garden. I was telling Connor and Fiona, David, that I've got a couple in my bedroom. Grandma bought them from her friend who did them a few years ago. They're pretty vile, but she liked them.' She laughed ruefully. 'Bless her. She had the most terrible taste in paintings.' She smiled. 'That reminds me. She showed me a whole trunk of old canvases in the attic last year, and wanted me to find out about them, but to be honest they just look like mud. I hadn't the heart to tell her. I must get round to throwing them out. They're really manky, and some of them have got mould on.'

David and Fiona exchanged glances, aghast. 'It might be worthwhile getting them looked at,' said David carefully, 'seeing as she worked for an art collector.'

'Really?' said Jane rather unbelievingly. 'Honestly, they're the most dreary things.'

Visions of the searing landscapes painted by war veterans in the Twenties filled David's imagination, along with the nightmare state of the attic, leaking and damp. He stifled his impatience. 'What do you think, Fiona?' he suggested.

Fiona spoke equally carefully. She had gone very white, and David thought that it was no wonder. In fact, he was surprised her hair hadn't turned grey on the spot.

'A lot of the painters that Doctor Macaulay looked after were pretty broken up by the war. Some of them did paint canvases that look like mud, especially at first. We know that Reamur and Elkmann did, because they wrote letters about it, but it's always been assumed that they destroyed those first attempts. I would get those canvases to Christie's in Edinburgh as soon as you can, if I were you, Jane. If the doctor left them to your grandparents, they might be extremely valuable. It's especially important if they're in bad condition. The sooner they get looked at, the better. And I wouldn't mention anything about this to anybody, including Connor.'

Jane looked at them both, surprised. 'Well, all right. I'll let you know what Christie's say. But I'm sure you're both wrong. Grandma would have told me if they were from Doctor Macaulay. She was so proud of him.'

Perhaps she didn't like the paintings he'd given her and was embarrassed about that, thought Fiona. But she hardly liked to argue the point with her cousin.

Jane, dismissing the subject, returned to one that interested her much more. 'Well, anyway, I just hate to think of Connor Macaulay sitting in Shaws planning to swallow up my home.'

Fiona smiled. 'Given that he would like the property, wouldn't it have been hypocritical of him if he'd made an offer through an agent so that you wouldn't realise it was him?'

Jane dumped a handful of forks into the cutlery drawer. 'He had no right to make an offer at all!'

'The people who live below me have just told me they'd like to buy my flat when I move,' said David. 'I rather appreciated it, actually. It certainly hasn't made me feel as if they're predators. Apart from anything else, it'll save on agency fees.'

'He knows how much I love this place — when he came here, I spent half the evening going on about it! No one could ever make any offer that would tempt me to sell.'

'Well, if he hadn't realised it before yesterday evening, he has now, hasn't he?' said David dryly. 'Lots of people love their homes, but I suspect that most people in your position would think long and hard about the sort of offer you got from him. Twice the market value of this place — why, just the interest on your profit in the first few years would pay for the start-up of your business!'

Jane stopped for a moment, the tea towel still in her hand, diverted. 'Would it really?'

Fiona laughed. 'Honestly, Jane, for someone who did a maths degree . . .'

'Well, everyone knows houses in Scotland are terribly cheap,' said Jane defensively.

David grinned. 'You know that road bridge they've just announced they're going to build across the Forth? A cottage in Elie with two bedrooms and a tiny garden went for thousands last week. All the Edinburgh hotshots are looking to buy around here now because they'll be able to drive their classy cars into work.'

Fiona grimaced. 'We know far too much about house prices round here since yesterday.' She turned to Jane. 'We started going to solicitors to try to find a place for when David gets back from the States. All I can say is that it's lucky David's such a disgustingly well-paid lawyer, or we wouldn't have a chance to buy a thing.'

Jane seized the chance to change the topic of conversation and asked about how they had fared. As she had hoped, they rose to the bait willingly and were soon talking eagerly about various possibilities. Pleased that they were planning to buy nearby, she was genuinely glad to be able to concentrate on something else for a while, rather than the vexed question of what Connor was up to.

Once they'd had coffee, she excused herself to have a long soak in the bath. She'd only had time for a quick shower when she got in last night, and wanted to take time to nurse her foot and lose herself for a while in a cloud of bubbles and scent.

In the bathroom, wafts of steam eddying around her, and her favourite bath essence already swirling in the water, she hung up her robe on the door and caught her hair up to the top of her head with a couple of combs.

Unwinding the bandage round her

ankle, she was pleased to see that the swelling had subsided considerably. It had really not been such a bad fall after all. It felt stiff and uncomfortable, but she was able to walk on it unaided today, unlike some previous occasions when she had hardly been able to set her foot to the ground for a few days.

Easing herself into the bath, she started to feel more relaxed almost at once. She sighed. Perhaps things weren't so bad. It was an ill wind that blew no good at all. At least she had the offer of a very good salary until September, which would put her a long way towards a solid financial foundation for her business.

She'd be able to save all of it, and could use some of it to get the big work done in the garden as well as initial advertising costs. She hoped to build her business mostly through word of mouth and personal recommendation, but a medium-sized, properly set half-page in the local telephone directory would be very useful, and it was the sort of thing that she wouldn't otherwise be able to afford for a few months.

Of course, she hastily reminded herself, she didn't definitely intend to take up the job offer!

★ ★ ★

David was able to tell her about Connor by lunchtime. He'd contacted his friend by telephone, while Jane was in the bath.

'Apparently Connor is the main mover and shaker for the whole Macaulay enterprise,' said David. 'Robin says that after Doctor Macaulay moved to the States, his family became enormously wealthy because of buying and selling artworks, and then because of property speculation in Boston. There's a collection of paintings in the original Boston mansion, and there's always some on public show there as the Macaulay Collection — it's a museum. Robin says it works out pretty well for the family taxes.'

Jane screwed up her face in an effort

of concentration. 'So where exactly does Connor fit into this?'

'Connor has a private income from family money. But it wasn't until his father retired two years ago that he started overseeing the management of the collection. Robin doesn't know exactly what he did before that, except that he had an MBA at Harvard, and managed investments for the family. He did a crash course in art history at the Sorbonne, though, before taking over from his father — flew back and forth to Paris for the whole of '55.'

'Well, that explains why he's so knowledgeable about art in general — I was impressed with that!' said Fiona.

David looked quizzically at Jane. 'Robin also said that a while ago Connor visited the old family estate in Scotland out of sheer curiosity, was very taken with it, and made the absentee owners of the main house an offer they couldn't refuse. The last he heard, he was hoping to have the same luck with the owner of the rest of the property.'

Jane clenched her fists involuntarily. 'I'll show him there are some things that money can't buy!'

'Well, at least I don't see anything in what Robin said that should stop you taking up Connor's job offer,' said Fiona reasonably.

Jane sighed. 'I suppose so. What do you think, David?'

'I agree with Fiona.' He paused. 'If you don't do it, somebody else will snap it up.'

Jane thought for a moment. 'Well, I'll take the rest of the weekend to think about it a bit more. But that's a really important point. You mean I can't change the situation; I might as well make the most of it.'

But despite these brave words, Jane still found it difficult to shift her gloomy mood, which was matched by the weather. A strong breeze had driven up dark clouds from the west, and the first raindrops fell as she, Fiona and David were discussing what to do over the rest of the weekend.

This instantly changed their ideas. Jane had been vaguely thinking of potting up some seedlings in the greenhouse, and Fiona and David of walking along the coast path, but as the rain started to batter against the windows the girls thankfully accepted David's offer to take Pip for his walk, and settled down to a peaceful afternoon indoors.

It was the first day for over a month that Fiona had been at home and not working flat out; and Jane, idly rocking in the corner with her foot on a stool and letters to write, was pleased to see her curl up on the sofa with a pencil and the Scotsman crossword. Doing the crossword together was a childhood game of theirs, which they hadn't played for ages.

'Ready, Jane?'

'You know perfectly well I ought to be writing these letters!'

'OK, Here goes! One down. Opinion in France. Seven letters.'

Jane laughed. 'Easy-peasy. Comment.'

'Brilliant! Now count to five and let

me think first on this one. Three down. Eyes ahoy. Seven letters.'

Jane was just about to start counting when the phone rang. Fiona hopped up to answer. Jane took up her pen to continue her letter, but froze as she heard Fiona's clear voice.

'Why, how kind of you to call, Connor!'

Jane's insides seemed to flip over and she gestured frantically at Fiona, shaking her head emphatically. Fiona smiled at her as she listened intently into the receiver, cocking her head slightly with the courteous attention it was second nature for her to give.

'She's fine, thank you, and said her foot was much better today. I'll tell her you called. Would you like her to call you back? I'm not sure when that would be.' She listened again attentively, and laughed. Jane looked at her own hands clasping and unclasping on her lap, and her pen fallen on the floor, with curious detachment.

'One last thing — seven letters

— eyes ahoy — yes, you destroyed my train of thought — of course! Thank you! Bye, then.' She put down the phone and hopped up onto the sofa again, grinning at Jane as she filled in the answer. 'Care to find out what he said?'

★ ★ ★

The next morning dawned bright and windy; the high winds overnight had evidently blown the rainclouds away. The wind in her face was fresh and invigorating as Jane walked, limping only slightly, along the footpath that wended its way on the edge of the wood around the back of the village. She had slept well and woken up feeling a good deal better about Connor's startling suggestions. After all, she conceded grudgingly, it had been very good of him to ring up the next day to enquire after her injured ankle.

The footpath was a shorter and much prettier route than the main road. She could easily manage it after resting her ankle yesterday. She was going to the nine o'clock early service. Fiona and David had only just got up, and they would appreciate having the place to themselves for an hour.

Once inside the porch, the quietness of the old kirk was even more pronounced than usual as the wind stopped buffeting around her. She smiled at Mrs Anderson, handing out hymnals just inside the door, and walked down the side aisle to the seat she'd used ever since she was a little girl. As she sat down she remembered with a shudder the pins and needles she suffered from during long services as a child, her legs not long enough to rest her feet on the floor. Grandma and Grandpa had always been sticklers for the strictest behaviour in the kirk.

Taking off her beret, she ran her hand through her hair to free up the curls from the confines of a hat. She tried to quieten her mind in preparation for the service, but she could not stop thinking about the events of yesterday.

Talking with Fiona yesterday afternoon, she had realised that at least she might be able to soften the worst disasters of an ultramodern house conversion. Only last year a similar conversion in the village had ended up with a collapsed inner wall when builders hadn't realised it was loadbearing. Moreover, she'd decided that if Shaws were to be stripped, it would be better to see it done than to spend the next few months visualising the worst and not seeing what was going on.

Having said that, she was determined to find out as much as she could about what the job would entail before agreeing to take on such a responsibility. She could imagine all sorts of scenarios taking place if he were so minded. Thinking about them again, she shuddered.

Supposing he argued that she'd overstepped her brief and threatened to sue for the costs of redoing work she'd countenanced but he disapproved of?

Perhaps the whole scheme was a set-up to put her in debt — or legal liability — to him, so that she'd end up forced to sell the cottage! Putting these points to David yesterday, she was secretly rather dismayed when, far from scoffing, he treated her concerns quite seriously and counselled her to ensure that her responsibilities were written down and her work closely minuted.

She sighed. It was starting to look as if she would be really earning this enormous salary. She'd envisaged popping over once or twice a day to make coffee and chat to the people working on the building in a low-key approach.

She'd said as much to David. He'd laughed. 'Well, that's what it will consist of,' he'd said. 'It's just that you'll need to record the relevant bits of your chats. You'll be acting as a go-between; you need to make absolutely certain that the communication about what's going on is as clear as possible between Connor and the people working on the house.'

The organ stopped playing and the

choir rose for the opening hymn. Jane pulled herself together sharply. She'd been sitting in the kirk for twenty minutes and all she'd done was to think about her own affairs. She forced herself to attend, and gradually became more and more engrossed in the quiet, measured worship that had been part of her life for so long.

At the end of the service she stayed in her seat for a few minutes, listening to the beautiful Bach chorale being played on the organ. The music completed that which the service had started; she felt at peace with herself and her fellow men, even American businessmen with a penchant for property dealings. She bent down to retrieve her hymnbook, which had fallen on the floor, and froze in shock as she straightened up.

Connor Macaulay was standing in the aisle. Clad in a charcoal-grey suit and white shirt with a tie exactly the colour of his eyes, he took her breath away. She could only nod silently as he smiled at her and asked if he might have a word for a minute.

He must have been to the service too. He must have been sitting behind her the whole time. She blushed at the thought, remembering how she had dropped her purse during the collection and scrabbled on the floor to pick up all the coins. That had been embarrassing enough, but the thought of Connor watching the whole scene was excruciating. Her temper flared, as it always did, and she spoke without thinking.

'Good morning. I must say I'm surprised to see you. I hadn't put you down as a churchgoer.'

To do him credit, the man didn't flinch. 'Well, some Americans do go to church, you know,' he said mildly. He smiled at her, and she had the grace to blush; to be sure, he didn't take offence easily. If only they weren't in such a public place! She could feel the eyes of the whole congregation boring into them in undisguised interest.

'It sure is good to see you, Jane. I was a little surprised to see you too; I had you confined indoors with that foot of yours for the next day or two.'

Jane gathered her scattered wits with a tremendous effort, thanked him for his concern, and bore her end of a polite exchange of comment on the beauty of the building, although she couldn't help noticing that the corner of Connor's mouth was twitching. Was he laughing at her again? Was he as aware of others' attention as she?

In fact she couldn't help noticing the rest of his mouth either. Or his eyes, looking at her, drawing her glance time and time again. And even at eleven in the morning, the planes of his jaw were shadowed; they only served to emphasise the untamed air that always seemed to be about him. He looked so strong. Kissing him would be a dangerous experience.

Shocked at herself for the direction her thoughts had taken, Jane dragged herself back to the conversation with an effort. They must get out of the kirk before the entire village had heard about a long intimate conversation after the service and drawn every sort of conclusion.

Having just decided she must not be seen talking to him any more, she found herself walking out of the door with him, introducing him to some who had not met him, together exchanging courtesies with others — this was even worse!

She had just made up her mind to make any excuse to get away when he looked down at her and smiled in that heart-stopping way he had. 'I forgot to ask,' he said. 'May I walk you home?' She laughed, and went through the gate that he had just opened for her. She had to hand it to him — he was a past master at manoeuvring.

As they walked along the path together, an uncharacteristic silence grew between them. Jane thought quickly. Now was the time to put the strategy that she had decided upon into practice — now, before things got any further.

Just as she had made up her mind to speak, Connor broke the silence. 'Jane,

I've been thinking about what I said to you yesterday, and about you and me — how we first met . . . I mean, all that misunderstanding at first . . . and I've never told you all about what I want to do with Shaws . . . ' As had happened once before, his voice had changed. Now it was hesitant, diffident; his fluency seemed to have deserted him. His face was turned away from her.

Oh no! He's really regretting having made that offer yesterday!

All at once Jane was aware of just how much she wanted the job he'd offered. She was careful to keep her tone light. 'Would you prefer to find someone else to work for you?'

Connor turned around quickly to her, and their eyes met for a moment, and held.

'I would like you to take up my offer of work,' he said slowly. 'That hasn't changed at all. No, there's something else I'd like to tell you, though you may think it's not really relevant, because it — well, it happened such a long time ago, it's — well, it's kind of a personal thing. I'd rather you didn't tell anybody else right now, but it might . . . '

Jane listened with a growing sense of exasperation. She had no wish to get involved in personal stories, some appeal to her good nature. *For Heaven's sake, you're a businessman! You wouldn't talk like this to one of your business colleagues. Stop trying to manipulate me!* It was imperative that she keep things on a strictly business-like footing, if there was to be any chance of this working. Good fences made good neighbours.

She broke in: 'You don't need to do that. I wanted to let you know that I've made up my mind about your offer of employment.' She went on carefully, remembering the strategy that she had thought out in detail. 'I'd probably like to take it up, but I'd like to find out exactly what it entails first, and have it down in writing, since you'll be away such a lot.'

Connor stopped and looked at her; she forced herself to look into his face, having assumed what she hoped came across as a bright, professional attitude.

'That's really good news,' he said enthusiastically. His diffidence seemed to melt away, and his eyes lit up as he smiled down at her. 'Perhaps you'd care to go out for dinner sometime in the next couple of days. We could discuss all this then . . . There's a new production of *As You Like It* on at the Edinburgh Playhouse; shall we go to it as well?'

Jane drew a deep breath. 'I would prefer things to be on a more formal basis. I have to be frank; I think it would really be best to keep things on a less personal level. There wouldn't really be any point in us discussing the changes you want to make. I would rather take them as given and make sure that they are implemented, unless I see practical difficulties.'

Connor looked at her quizzically. 'Are you sure that we differ so much on what we want for Shaws, Jane?'

Jane set her teeth. Exasperation flooded through her, but she spoke quietly, determined to keep calm.

'Well, for instance, I heard that you're aiming to take up the old planning permission for building on the estate. Is that true?'

'Well, yes, but . . . '

Jane cut him short. 'I think that's made my case, Connor. I would really rather not have to discuss this. Having said that, I can assure you that I would do the work efficiently and professionally.' She paused. 'Would you be happy with a more impersonal approach? I wouldn't be able to take it up otherwise.'

Connor was no longer smiling at her. His attitude, relaxed and open a moment ago, was immediately replaced; it was as if a switch marked 'Businessman' had been put on. He had been leaning slightly towards her; now he straightened up. It was the impersonal attitude she had asked for.

'Certainly,' he said in a professional, neutral tone. 'I'll have a draft proposal of the way I see the job working by tomorrow morning; perhaps I could post it to you, and you would have time

91

to look at it before deciding for certain one way or another.'

They were nearly back at the cottage; as they turned the last corner they abruptly came upon Bruce and Aileen with their two children, good friends of Jane's, ringing the doorbell for little Freya to say hello, as they usually did on their way to the family service.

Bruce Laird was a farmer who, before Aileen had moved to the village four years ago, had lived only for his Saturday afternoons as goalkeeper for the local football team. Jane had always been very fond of him, and had been so pleased when he'd become besotted with the petite, efficient, gentle accountant who never had a hair out of place.

Now Aileen's hair was always wildly rumpled by her boisterous little baby, and she looked relaxed and comfortable even in her dress for the kirk; while Bruce, in his best Sunday kilt, made a startling contrast to his filthy appearance yesterday. Jane had bumped into them at the greengrocer's, Bruce muddy but triumphant in his football kit, waiting outside with the baby while Aileen was buying a celebratory toffee apple for Freya.

Before Jane knew quite what had happened, she found herself introducing Bruce and Aileen. She could not look at Connor. Her whole face felt fiery and hot; she was sure everyone was looking at her, and wanted to sink into the ground.

A little hand stealing into hers reminded her of her goddaughter. Freya was always very keen on the proprieties, and she'd forgotten to include her in the introductions. 'This is Freya,' she said, hearing her own voice sounding unnaturally high and nervous. She felt fiercely protective towards the little girl, her hand so small and warm in hers, standing half-hidden behind her skirt. Freya was painfully shy with strangers.

Connor hunkered down, not too close, but so that his head was on a level with Freya's. Freya clutched Jane's hand harder, and put her thumb in her mouth. Connor looked at her and smiled. 'Your dress is pink. It's got blue flowers on it,' he said seriously.

Freya stared back at him. After a moment she took her thumb out of her mouth and lifted up one foot carefully towards him. 'I got my dress yesterday at Jenner's and I've got a puppy on my shoe. Look!' She clutched Jane's hand even tighter as she tried to show him the side of her little boot. 'This morning my little brother Jim wanted to ride on the cows, but I told him only big girls can do that,' she said with all the seriousness of a three-year old.

Connor tickled nine-month old James, kicking and laughing uproariously in his mother's arms. 'You're a little rascal, trying to bamboozle your sister like that!' he told him.

Jane could only stare, fascinated despite herself at the way Connor had established such an immediate rapport with the children. Now Freya was telling him what she'd had for breakfast, for goodness' sake! Prying Freya away from Connor so that she wouldn't be late for church would take some doing.

To her horror, Jane found that Freya was inviting Connor to tea next week. Before she could say a word, she realised that everyone was assuming she'd be coming too. Faced with the enthusiasm of Bruce and Aileen, and her goddaughter, she could hardly refuse, or start to explain to a toddler that she had a purely professional relationship with the toddler's new and wonderful friend and had firmly ruled out things like going to tea with him.

Luckily Connor solved the problem for her. 'Freya, I have to go away very soon, first to London and then back to my home in America,' he said. 'I won't be back for quite a while, but I would love to come to tea then. Is that OK?'

Freya was persuaded, and Jane smiled wryly. She looked at Bruce and Aileen. It was easy to see that they were pleased with Connor; unsurprising too, for it was only last week they and Jane had been talking about how few adults included children in a conversation.

She thought that it was a side to Connor Macaulay she'd never have expected. Wheeler-dealer, yes; suave businessman, yes; expert manipulator, yes — though he'd do it to her over her dead body! But a family man? Unwillingly, she had to admit that it only added to his charm. To be honest, she'd never met a man so attractive on the face of it.

She scowled at him, but he was blissfully oblivious to the fact. He had his back half-turned on her, but she could see his eyes crinkling as he smiled at her little goddaughter. At this rate he'd have the whole village under his thumb in a month, no matter what he did with Shaws. She'd have few allies in any battle against him.

Letter of 24 May 1958, Miss Jane Duncan to Mr Connor Macaulay.
Dear Mr Macaulay,
Thank you for your letter. I enclose the signed contract.

With best wishes for your stay in London,

Yours sincerely,

Jane Duncan.

Letter of 25 May 1958, Mr Connor Macaulay to Miss Jane Duncan.

Dear Miss Duncan,

Thank you for your letter. I have left a set of keys for you at the solicitor's; you will find the detailed plans in the master bedroom on the desk. I am sorry that we did not have time to go through them before I left. The builders are coming in at nine on Wednesday morning.

Yours,

Connor Macaulay.

5

On Monday morning, Jane told herself she was far too busy to go wandering round Shaws. In fact, Connor Macaulay would be lucky if she got the keys five minutes before the builders were due to arrive!

As she weeded energetically, Pip ambling about in the early morning sunshine, she mentally ticked off a list of all the things that needed to be done that week. Fiona had mentioned the canvasses again at breakfast, and she'd promised to take them to Edinburgh later this morning. The tree surgeon was coming that afternoon, and before then she was determined to clear heavy undergrowth away from some of the oldest trees to give Jane a chance to see the state of the trunks. It was likely that at least two of the trees would have to come out; she hoped that the soil would be in good enough condition to plant saplings in their stead. On the other hand, she strongly suspected a viral infection in the beech, which would mean she'd have to put any replanting on hold for a while.

Straightening for a moment to rub her aching back and flex her ankle — still slightly stiff despite a tightly wrapped bandage under her boot — she sighed. The greenhouses desperately needed attention, this week if possible. The plumbing in them was broken, several panes of glass were missing, and most of the windows were covered in mould. If she were to get any use out of them this year, they would have to be attended to fast.

At least the wood and iron structures were dry and sound, and would only need another coat of paint. Ron was coming round that afternoon to have a look. Perhaps they might be done by the end of the week, if she worked with him on them. But it would mean at least two trips to the local builder's merchants in the next couple of days. Perhaps Jamie could help out as well in the evenings; she'd better phone him later on.

Meanwhile, she'd have to call into the solicitors sometime today to pick up the keys for Shaws. Pulling at a particularly stubborn weed, she swore viciously as a hidden thorn sank into her finger. *Why on earth did I agree to this perfectly ridiculous scheme? I've more than enough to do already! And he didn't even have the common sense to drop a set of keys off with me, so I've got to waste time getting changed and cleaned up to see Mr McDougall!*

Conveniently forgetting that it was she who had insisted Connor leave the keys at the solicitors, to underline the professional nature of her dealings on his behalf, she swore again and Pip came up, whining softly and pushing his head under her hand for comfort. She stroked him absent-mindedly, sucking her finger in a vain attempt to get the thorn out. It was going to be a difficult day.

★ ★ ★

That evening the sun was sinking in a blaze of splendour, the sky a symphony of pink and green, but Jane was unable to appreciate it. She could not suppress an overwhelming feeling of sadness as she walked towards the wicket gate into the Shaws estate. This part of her garden had been a favourite spot in the past; now she was unable to feel at ease here. It had been a private place, but from now on anyone might be walking in the estate gardens, and they would be able to see her if she were here.

Looking at the lovely old trees of Shaws that rose above the walls of her garden, she knew she had to get used to the idea that it would all be changed soon anyway — just as she'd tried *not* to do with her own property. She grimaced as she thought of the hotel from which Connor was writing to her. The Dorchester, for heaven's sake! Though it had only been built twenty years ago, even the Scottish newspapers

101

had had lots of articles featuring the enormous redesign that it had just undergone.

Leaning on the wicket gate, looking at the weathered grey lines of the house she loved so well, she thought of the quiet, old-fashioned law office she'd been in that afternoon, with its orderly rows of case histories and well-worn furniture. It seemed to stand for all that she held dear, and all that a brash businessman would sweep away.

The hour she'd spent at the solicitors' had been even more uncomfortable than she had feared. Jane's heart sank lower as she thought about the effect the news had had on one of her grandparents' oldest friends.

Mr McDougall had looked at her soberly, his fingers steepled together as they always did when he was distressed. His kindly old face looked suddenly much older, his gentle Gaelic burr more pronounced.

'My dear, I am in a very difficult position, for is not the gentleman my own client? But I would not be true to myself if I did not tell you I'm not so happy with your position here. That is not to say that I am uneasy with Mr Macaulay himself. He seems a sound fellow. But as for what he is going to do with his property . . . Och, you know well how strongly you feel for your grandfather's work, and for the house of Shaws. Wheesht, girl, look at the car that the man is for driving!'

Jane had had to smile at that; Mr McDougall drove, very carefully and slowly, an Austin that had rolled off the production line in 1927. He was not the man to appreciate this year's Aston Martin.

Mr McDougall had got up stiffly and walked over to the window. He'd taken out a large handkerchief and blown his nose. Still looking out of the window, he'd cleared his throat. 'My dear, you know how fond I was of your granny and grandpa. I would not like to think that you were put into an uncomfortable position by money problems. If it is a question of financial difficulties you're in . . . '

Jane closed her eyes. It had been very uncomfortable. She'd had to try to make him understand why she was taking up the job, and understand that she wasn't just doing it for the money.

Half an hour later, the old solicitor still hadn't been completely convinced, but at least he wasn't as upset as he had been earlier. She knew the tremendous amount of guilt he was labouring under; a few years ago he had tried to buy Shaws from the English firm himself. Then he had withdrawn his offer when interest rates unexpectedly took a hike, worried that the mortgage would put him under too large a financial obligation. But he still worried that he would have been able to manage very well, and he and Jane both knew it, though the subject remained unspoken between them.

As Jane opened the wicket gate there was a mad flurry of paws and tail, and Pip scrambled through, racing into the gardens in an ecstasy of delight, barking madly and chasing imaginary birds as if he was a puppy again. Jane couldn't imagine what had got into him. He had been quite happy gently snuffling around rose bushes two minutes before. He was far too old to behave like this!

Calling Pip had no effect at all and in the end Jane had to sneak up on him and drag him, protesting, back to the gate. But Pip looked so doleful, staring through the wrought iron rails, that Jane took pity on him. She marched back to the cottage and retrieved Pip's lead from the porch, secretly rather relieved to have put off the moment of going into Shaws for a few minutes at least.

Fiona called through from the kitchen in surprise. 'Back already, Jane? That was quick! Come and have some tea.'

Jane sighed. It was very tempting. Then she shook herself mentally. *For goodness' sake, this isn't a big deal!* 'No, I just forgot Pip's lead. He wants to come exploring too, but I'll have to tie him up outside the house.'

Fiona appeared, wiping her hands on a kitchen towel. 'Is he being difficult? Do you want me to keep him inside?' She looked at Jane and added, 'Or I could pop over with you, and keep Pip from going frantic while you're in the house? The dinner's able to look after itself for an hour now.'

Jane accepted gladly. She felt quite unreasonably nervous about going into the house that held so many memories for her and which she had not entered for so long.

The two girls walked back across the grass in silence, and even Pip was uncharacteristically quiet. Unconsciously Jane rubbed her thumb against the carved wooden cat on the key ring she'd picked up from Mr McDougall that afternoon, the very keys her grandparents had always had. Grandma had always said that set of keys had been her favourite pram toy.

'By the way, how did it go at Christie's this morning?' asked Fiona.

'Oh, all right,' replied Jane absently. 'They took them, at least, but they did the same for an old lady next to me who'd brought in a load of plastic teaspoons! They said they'd let me know within the next few weeks.'

She became aware that she was trembling as she fitted the key to the old oak door. It turned easily. 'I'll stay here; you take your time,' said Fiona. Jane smiled at her cousin and, turning, walked into the hall.

Dust motes danced and whirled in the air around her, golden in the last rays of the sun that streamed through the open doorway. That same languorous light suffused the whole hall, the wooden floors, and the beautiful sweep of stairs up to the high arched windows above. Astounded, she breathed in the air more carefully to check if she could really smell that lavender beeswax polish her grandma had always used. Surely not; Grandma hadn't been in the house for fifteen years. She shook her head. It was definitely there, and what was more, the floor had obviously been polished recently. But she hadn't heard of anybody being called in to clean the house!

She hurried through the hall and along the corridor, past the library door, to the kitchen. With every step she took her astonishment grew. Everything was dusted and polished. In the kitchen the oil-fired Rayburn stove in the corner had a row of clean tea-towels draped above it, and under the scrubbed wooden draining board and scoured stone sink was a workmanlike box of cleaning materials including that beeswax polish and old-fashioned scouring soap that they'd always used.

The larder was stocked with biscuits, sugar, tea, coffee and tins of evaporated milk. A new coffeepot and a new kettle stood by the sink, and a simple gas ring attached to a gas cylinder had been installed for times when the Rayburn was not being used. There was a note on the kitchen table for the people working on the house, inviting them to help themselves for tea and coffee breaks. Jane couldn't believe it.

Leaving the kitchen, she retraced her steps slowly to the library and opened the door tentatively. This was all exactly as she had remembered it — rather shabby, but again, spotlessly clean. The old chintz covers on the sofas were as threadbare as ever. There was the worn leather chair in the corner. And there was the desk, positioned so that whoever was working could see out of the tall French windows, past the lovely sweep of lawn, up to the rockery and the glimpse of hills beyond.

Mr McDougall had always had the house checked regularly and regular repairs set in hand; but as Jane went through the empty, echoing rooms, she saw that the years had taken their toll. Damp had started to infiltrate the scullery and one of the bedrooms upstairs. The new owner had evidently not yet touched some of the rooms, and the furniture was still swathed in dust sheets and cobwebs. But the hall, the library, the kitchen — these three rooms had been attended to with the utmost consideration. By Connor himself, evidently.

Shaking her head in disbelief, Jane crossed the landing upstairs to the master bedroom. As she walked in, it was immediately clear that this was the one Connor had used; it was cleaned and polished with the now almost familiar care and attention she'd noticed elsewhere.

She suddenly realised that Connor had brought hardly any of his own things to the house. This room was furnished extremely simply, as was the whole house. Andrew Macaulay had sold the house furnished, and he had had a telephone put in — essential for a doctor — but he had not been a wealthy man before moving to America. His habit of buying paintings, as well as accepting poorer patients and treating them for free, had put paid to that. Successive owners had added nothing, and neither had Connor. No electricity, no radio, no gramophone, no television. The only new items Jane had seen in the whole house were in the kitchen. Remembering the old kettle and range, she could hardly blame him for that. He had left hardly any personal items in the house at all. She was amazed at how simply he must have lived, and how hard he must have worked at the house, during the few weeks he had been there. It didn't square with her image of him at all.

Looking at the desk for the papers he had mentioned, a book and a photograph in a simple wooden frame caught her eye. The photograph was of Connor with a young man, a young woman, and a child. They were all dressed in what looked like South American local clothes, sitting on a bench outside a rough hut, all laughing and smiling at the camera, their arms around each other, the little girl sitting on Connor's lap. Perhaps it was a family he was helping. She was touched; she wouldn't have put him down as being particularly interested in poor folk.

On impulse she crossed over and

picked it up. He had evidently left the book behind. It wasn't a book from the library downstairs, but a modern copy of one of her favourite poets, Donne. Without really thinking, she turned over the pages and found herself softly speaking the words aloud.

> *I wonder, by my troth, what thou,*
>   *and I*
> *Did, till we loved?*
> *If ever any beauty I did see,*
> *Which I desired, and got, 'twas but*
>   *a dream of thee.*

After a moment she raised her head and looked towards the window, carefully replacing the book. His possessions were none of her business. Her own words to him came back to her. 'Would you be happy with a more impersonal approach? I wouldn't be able to take the job up otherwise.'

The plans were on the desk, as he'd said, and she sat down to look at them in the gathering dusk. It wasn't until she had nearly finished reading that she started to take in their import. She got to the end of the closely written sheets and flicked through them again.

The work Connor had arranged for would respect and enhance Shaws immeasurably. He had evidently been over the house with a fine-toothed comb. Nothing had been overlooked; everything had been planned for its repair and renovation. It was clear that no money was to be spared; but in a way that would make the house look as it had done in its prime, under the loving attention of her grandparents.

But there was more to it than this. Connor was planning to renovate Shaws not just for himself, but for others too. The holiday homes were three beautiful little log cabins in remote parts of the estate, for families to come and stay. The rundown old stables were to be rebuilt as an administrative block. The old house was to be kept by Connor, but the rest was to become part of the charity arm of the Macaulay Foundation, run primarily to care for families whose lives were still shattered by the war — children who had lost parents; refugees who, now that they finally were able to leave camps, had no home to return to; wounded soldiers and their families, still suffering from the effects of the desperate struggle against Hitler.

And I refused to listen to Connor when he wanted to discuss his plans! I assumed so much!

She suddenly realised that the papers were shaking in her hand. She was trembling all over.

A flurry of barks roused her from her reverie and she went to the window to see Pip and Fiona below on the lawn. Fiona was throwing sticks for Pip, laughing as Pip lumbered after them with all the speed of a sloth. She suddenly realised that she had been in the house for over an hour and it was very nearly dark. If she stayed any longer, she would have to start lighting gas mantles and let Fiona and Pip inside.

Slowly replacing the plans on Connor's desk, she looked around the familiar room one last time before closing the door gently and going downstairs. In the fast-gathering darkness her footsteps seemed louder, the house larger and more full of echoes. She still felt slightly dazed. She had entered Shaws to say farewell to the house as she'd known it. Now she was leaving in the knowledge that it was going to be given a new lease of life.

Outside, Pip stopped chasing sticks as soon as he saw her. He was a very old dog, but he came as fast as he could, as if she'd been away for years. She knelt down and hugged him, glad to hide her face from Fiona for a few seconds at least. She didn't know quite what to say to her.

Fiona looked at her, a slim figure in the dusk, her hair tumbled about Pip, murmuring endearments into one floppy ear. Her heart went out to her. *You've had enough to put up with all your life, Jane. You didn't need all this as well.*

It's such a shame; I thought you and Connor were made for each other.

She remembered the first Christmas after Jane had come to live with them, when they were both just ten. They'd put out their stockings the night before, but as they were opening them together she had looked at Jane and been shocked to see tears rolling down her cheeks. Fiona had tried offering her a chocolate, but it hadn't worked. She could still remember how Jane had confessed, after much coaxing, that she'd had a dream just before she woke up. She had dreamt that her parents weren't dead after all; and just for a moment, in that twilight world between sleeping and waking, she'd thought it was true.

★ ★ ★

To Jane's surprise — and gratitude — Fiona heard about the plans with admirable restraint. She neither volunteered an opinion on Connor's motives, nor commented on Jane's agitation, but merely asked her whether the plans made her feel easier about having Connor as a neighbour.

Jane frowned in thought. 'I think so. It doesn't change the fact that he wants my cottage. But . . . yes. Yes, of course. It'll make my job at Shaws much easier — well, it'll be lovely.' Her slim hands twisted about each other.

Or it would've been lovely if you hadn't got completely the wrong end of the stick about what Connor was going to do with the house, and insulted him into the bargain, thought Fiona dryly.

'In effect, it's giving me the chance to help with what I've always wanted to do with Shaws,' said Jane. She paused and looked at Fiona. 'There's another bit I haven't told you about. He's asked me to submit plans for the garden. Recreating it as his grandfather had it. Using the same types of plants as much as possible. And he hasn't even mentioned a budget!'

Fiona whistled. The two of them

walked back together in thoughtful silence.

Letter from Miss Jane Duncan to Mr Connor Macaulay, 24 May 1958.
Dear Mr Macaulay,
I looked at your plans yesterday. An apology is in order. I am bound to say that I like them very much.
Yours sincerely,
Jane Duncan.

Letter from Mr Connor Macaulay to Miss Jane Duncan, 25 May 1958.
Dear Miss Duncan,
Thank you for your letter. There is absolutely no need to apologise. I am delighted that you approve of the plans for Shaws, and look forward to your formal proposal for the garden renovations.
Yours sincerely,
Connor Macaulay.

Jane stared at the message. A cold stone seemed to settle in her stomach.

She leant down to scratch Pip behind the ears. 'Well, I've succeeded in making a really good friend there, old boy!' she said softly.

She found it very difficult to sleep that night. Plans for the Shaws estate — hadn't she made them a thousand times already? Jostled with the immense number of jobs that needed doing at home and in the garden, and images of the rooms she'd explored yesterday. Over and above them all lingered the image of that man whom she hadn't been able to forget since that very first morning.

Tossing and turning in her bed, trying to find a cool part of her pillow to rest her hot forehead, she had to admit to herself that she had been wrong about Connor. Yes, his offer still stood to buy her cottage; but now, knowing what he wanted to do with Shaws, she could even feel sympathy towards his attempt to recreate his grandfather's house in its entirety. By now she was also fairly sure that he was practical and pragmatic enough to let the matter rest. He would not try to change her mind.

She admired Connor. She would even like to be his friend. But she had ruined any chance of a personal relationship between them. What was it that he had wanted to tell her after church on Sunday? She remembered his hesitant words: *It happened a long time ago . . . it's kind of a personal thing . . .* She would never find out now. As she thought of the quiet, bitter words she'd flung at him like little stones, her face flamed again and again.

Eventually she got up. It was still terribly early, but she couldn't face her thoughts any longer. She showered and dressed, getting some comfort from the sensations of shampoo and soap, the soft touch of warm towels, and a sleepy welcome from Pip, who had been curled up next to the stove. It all helped her to think more positively. At least she might be able to salvage her self-respect by doing a sound professional job for him. He might even accept her suggestions for the garden!

She made a quick breakfast and went into the garden while it was still grey dawn, lugging a bucket of hot soapy water and the materials she'd bought yesterday for cleaning up the greenhouse. As she started to scrub the paintwork, she smiled to herself. Come what may, her garden would always be there for her.

Two hours and several buckets of detergent later, the greenhouse was transformed. It stood gently drying in the first sunlight of the day, ready to be painted by Jamie tomorrow. Jane felt an immense sense of satisfaction. It was a job she'd thought would take most of the morning. Her sleepless night had one good outcome at least.

Now she would be able to use the next few hours to walk round the Shaws estate with a notebook, and draft a proposal for Connor before he had time to change his mind about asking her to tender for the garden renovations. No, that wasn't fair. She had to admit that he had proved trustworthy. But a rapid professional response would show him how seriously she took this opportunity.

Without any more ado, she ran into the cottage, grabbed a pencil and her garden notebook, and whisked out again before Pip realised where she was going. Pip was snoozing comfortably by the range again — he'd gone back to the cottage earlier, exhausted by his early morning outing — and Jane had no intention of being distracted by him on this walk.

By the time Fiona and David had emerged and were having breakfast, Jane was back at the cottage, her head spinning with all the ideas that she'd jotted down and notes she had made to herself. The project was undoubtedly more than she could reasonably expect to land at this point in her career as a gardener. She was astute enough to realise that on several points she would have to call in outside help. Bill the tree surgeon would be indispensable. She also knew the person she would need to ask advice from on the species of plants most common in the Nineties, when James Macaulay had originally planned the garden. Many of the shrubs were still there, but had reached the natural end of their life. They would have to be replaced. She would need to find as many specialist organic seed and plant nurseries as possible. They would be most appropriate for sourcing the older varieties of plants that she required.

Between mouthfuls of toast and marmalade, she tried to explain something of her plans to Fiona and David. They looked slightly bemused by her unusual eloquence at half past eight in the morning. 'Of course, all he's asked me for are proposals, but it's nice to have the chance to make them. It's good practice, if nothing else.' She poured more coffee. 'I need to walk round the gardens again after breakfast to get the outline of my plans clear before I write them this morning. Would you mind coming with me so I could bounce my ideas off you?'

Jane waved her hand towards the rockery. 'It's pretty overgrown, and a lot of the more exotic plants have died, but you can see the original idea pretty clearly; the way old Doctor Macaulay planned it so that the view from his desk draws the eye upwards and outwards to the woods and the sky. The rockery's a deliberate way of moving your attention away from the formal lawn to the rocks and the hills beyond.' She gestured to the juniper trees against the sky, bent and aged with the sea winds.

They had come to the end of the tour round the estate, and were walking back towards the wicket gate, when she caught sight of a man walking from the outbuildings on the other side of the main building. He had evidently just arrived; he was stripping off his coat and coming towards them. It was too late to do anything about it. Before Jane could say a word, Fiona and David had noticed him as well, and Fiona had told David who it was.

Their paths intersected, and within moments they were together. Their eyes met; and for Jane, for a heartbeat, the world stopped, and she had to look away. She was unable to say a word. *You're not here! You 're in London!* She'd had a letter from him only yesterday afternoon, and he hadn't mentioned any change of plan.

Stealing a glance at him, and looking again, she suddenly knew, her heart beating painfully, that this man affected her as no one had ever done before. He was talking to David — she could see tiny laughter lines at the corners of his eyes — and she thought, *I've always known those were there.*

His face was as familiar to her as her own. She knew, without having to look, how his hands were dug deep into his pockets; how his shoulders were set square and uncompromising; how his eyes flared so quickly into amusement, sometimes cynical, sometimes unselfconscious. Listening to his deep voice, she knew how his quick wit ran ahead of the conversation so that his words, however slowly delivered, were always unerringly acute; and how his understanding meant that sometimes he didn't even have to speak to make one feel understood.

She slowly dragged herself back to the conversation, dimly aware that they had all been politely conversing for some time. He was being so formal! He wasn't even looking at her! She sighed.

' . . . I arranged leave with the trustees, so that means I can be here for the next three or four months.'

Jane was brought back to earth with a bump. If Connor were here, he wouldn't need her anymore. Just one thing was crystal clear — she didn't want the indignity of being 'let go'. She would rather do the resigning herself and keep her self-esteem intact. She spoke right away, before she had time to regret it.

'I'm thinking, Connor, since you'll be here in person . . . ' She kept the tone light and matter-of-fact. ' . . . you'll prefer to do the work I was going to do for the estate?' Try as she might, she couldn't keep a wobble from her voice at the end. She'd really started to appreciate how important the job was to her. Fiona noticed, of course — she looked quickly, sympathetically, at her — but to her intense relief, Connor didn't seem to register. She devoutly hoped not, and planted a bright smile on her face. 'Oh, you don't need to let me know immediately, but please don't feel obliged — '

Connor broke in: 'I still won't be able to oversee the whole thing; provide that continuity with builders and decorators. I'd really appreciate you carrying on.' He looked at her seriously, and held her gaze.

She was listening intently, but she could hardly take in the meaning of his words. Eventually she started to tune in. He was explaining that he needed to make trips to London and wouldn't be able to stay on site.

Fiona was looking at their faces. She

saw that Connor and Jane were speaking quite seriously, both standing back a little, unsure, polite. But their eyes were so much more eloquent; they were speaking a language without words. She felt David's hand tighten on hers, and she knew that he had noticed too.

6

There were cobwebs in Connor's hair, and his old jeans and shirt were grimy with dust. He'd been up in the attic all morning, lugging about and sorting through old packing cases of books they'd found a week ago.

'I've got the boxes unpacked and brought the books downstairs, so I've time to take Pip out and swing by Ceres Farm for that linchpin.'

Jane dragged herself away from the column of numbers in front of her with difficulty. She was in the middle of dealing with the insurance costs of the garden statues and sculptures. She glanced round to smile and nod briefly at the dishevelled figure in the doorway before going back to the paperwork.

It only took her a few more minutes to finish. Putting the papers in a file, with the analysis of costings she'd made on top, she jumped up from the desk and, stretching, went over to look out over the garden. It was raining hard; opening the French windows into the study, the air felt washed, cool and fresh. She couldn't wait to get out into the garden that afternoon, after the long deskbound morning. The heavy landscaping work being done around the pond should be over by the end of the day, and would show her whether it would be possible for her design to have the eventual effect she was aiming for, based on paintings of the pond from the Twenties.

She heard the side door open and saw Connor setting off across the lawn past the rockery, running, still in his filthy clothes and beat-up old shoes. Pip was scampering excitedly beside him. They would both be completely soaked by the time they got back.

She had to smile. So while she'd been sitting at a desk with a cup of coffee and a packet of chocolate biscuits all morning, congratulating herself on staying dry and warm indoors, he was bored by lifting boxes of books for hours, and was off for a four-mile run in the rain. She had to hand it to him; she prided herself on her energy, but his was amazing.

And he was so full of contradictions. After her first tour of the house — was it really only two weeks ago? — she had imagined that he was one of those super-tidy males who couldn't bear to have anything out of place. Certainly, when visitors were coming, he ensured the house was spotless. But from day to day he was as untidy as she was!

The kitchen had to be seen to be believed after little Freya came over one afternoon with the rest of her family in tow. He'd become Freya's idol forever after suggesting she might like to make some buns for tea, and together — allowing Jane in the kitchen only on condition she didn't help — they'd ended up making some very flat and solid scones, which Freya had declared were the best she'd ever tasted. It had taken them an hour and a half to clear up the enthusiastic cooks' efforts after the tea party!

And then there was the way he loved the most modern and up-to-date things — like his taste in hotels, cars, and movies — but appreciated the old as well. In practice he was keener than she to keep the house just as it was. And she'd accused him of wanting to modernise Shaws out of all recognition!

She sighed. After that disastrous conversation when she'd also insisted on a formal and wholly professional relationship, all traces of that extra warmth she'd known before had completely disappeared. Granted, while they had been working together he'd slowly become less formal — as he would be bound to under the circumstances. No one could stay completely formal when he was filthily muddy, or helping someone in and out of cobwebby attics!

And she could swear that he really enjoyed being with her — the renovations, choosing furnishings, developing designs . . . certainly they always seemed to work well together. She was putting in about twenty hours a week for him, and was now involved with every aspect of the renovations. He obviously trusted her judgement and respected her abilities.

But he insisted that she keep a timesheet that detailed every moment she spent on Shaws, and was punctilious about payment, adding an hourly rate to the retainer she was getting from him. He'd even insisted on paying for the time she'd been over for Freya's tea party, and had politely but firmly reminded her of the professional terms of their relationship when she protested. Her cheeks grew hot at the thought.

It all pointed to one thing. While she had grown to like him very much, and would have liked them to have at least become good friends and neighbours, he had remained distant. He treated her courteously and professionally, certainly, and was perfectly friendly, but as if he wouldn't like her as a particularly *close* friend. She and Fiona had both invited him for supper at the cottage, but he'd politely declined each time. And whenever he held her hand — which he had to do from time to time, crawling into lofts, over roofs, or up ladders — it was in the most impersonal way.

Jane shook her head firmly. Going back to the desk, she forced her attention back to another tranche of paperwork. The quotations from the specialist paint firms had finally all arrived, and she settled down to check the figures before Connor went over them that afternoon.

She jumped. Connor had returned, and was just outside the window. Turning to him, she saw that he was transformed. His dark hair was tousled and soaked through with rain; those long, thick eyelashes thwarting rivulets of water that ran down onto his face. His eyes snapped and sparkled as he grinned at her.

Jane dropped her eyes, only to find herself mesmerised by the sight of the raindrops clinging to his hands and his long, lean, tanned, muscular legs. She found herself thinking that he looked wild — yes, untamed — full of latent power. Her heart turned over.

'Shall I make lunch today, since you did yesterday?' he asked.

He smiled at her, and she retorted without thinking, furious at herself for her unexpected physical reaction to his appearance. 'For goodness' sake, wash and change before you even think about getting lunch ready!'

'Salami on rye suit you? Or I could make some tuna mayonnaise.' The last part of the sentence was muffled as Connor grasped the bottom of his soaking shirt in both hands and peeled it off. Jane's eyes widened involuntarily at the sight: hard outlines of ribs under the warm glow of his skin . . . his body stretching as he drew up his shirt in one lithe motion . . . the intense shadowing under his arms and over his chest

. . . the way stray raindrops played over the muscles of his arms . . .

Swallowing hard, and summoning up her best professional smile, Jane clenched her pen and managed to produce a spoken response, even if it sounded more of a croak than a proper sentence. 'Whatever — both sound good to me . . .'

But Connor had already turned to go into the house through the side door. He called to her from the hall: 'I promise I'll clean up before I get lunch — and after!'

She could hear him clattering along the corridor and up the stairs, whistling, his running shoes doubtless leaving more muddy footmarks as he went into the bathroom. The door closed; she heard the shower being turned on.

She forced her attention back to her work. *Damn! I should have written them down!* She hated to admit it to herself, but the sight of her employer had driven the cost derivatives she'd just calculated clean out of her head!

Jumping up to slam the French

windows shut with quite unnecessary force, she muttered ferociously under her breath. If anything were needed to underline his attitude towards her, that little scene had just done it. It was obvious she held no attraction for him. The sight of his stripping off in the rain might have overcome her just now, but it was all matter-of-fact to him. He showed not the slightest interest in her as a *woman* — not anymore. She could just as well be his sister! Well, she thought gloomily, it wasn't really surprising. She'd made it very clear to him, right at the start that she wasn't interested. She had very deliberately extinguished any slight spark of attraction he might have felt then.

It wasn't surprising that she felt attracted to him. It had to be admitted that he was really very good-looking. And so friendly, too. He'd certainly got all the women in Crail eating out of his hand within a couple of weeks. She'd caught Aileen and Fiona — who both had perfectly wonderful men of their own — raving about him to each other last week. Even Miss McIntosh, who found newcomers to the village so unnerving, had spent twenty minutes after church the other day telling Jane what a nice young man he was. Meanwhile, no one could exactly call her a siren. She spent far too much time with her face muddy!

After forcing herself to finish off the paperwork, she slowly got up and went to the kitchen, feeling strangely reluctant. Since starting to work for Connor, though she was very aware that she was attracted to him, she hadn't had any difficulty in treating him in a perfectly ordinary way. But the sight of him just now had really thrown her. She couldn't get that image of him out of her mind.

She opened the kitchen door to find him speaking on the telephone. She waited till he had finished, then went in. 'Can I do anything to help?'

He turned to welcome her with that endearingly lopsided smile. 'No, just pull up a chair — it's all nearly ready. That was Ron on the phone just now. He wants to go through the safety rules for the tractors he's bringing in tomorrow, so I suggested he lunch with us. He'll be over in a few minutes.' He turned back to the worktop.

Jane stared at his back. Something inside her seemed to be melting, and her insides were turning into jelly, not to mention her knees. She got to a chair and sat down fast.

As Connor turned round, she was suddenly caught by the sight of his capable, long fingers as he brought glassware and dishes to the table. His hands took up all her attention. It was impossible to drag her eyes away from them, let alone think about the rest of him. She remembered dimly having noticed his hands before, but she now realised she hadn't appreciated them at all.

Connor put a jug of water on the table, stopped, and looked at her more closely. 'Are you all right, Jane?' he asked, a shade of anxiety crossing his face. 'You're looking pretty out of it. Did you spend too long on the books?'

Jane was vaguely aware of him saying something, but was more struck by the delightful tone of his voice. Those liquid American vowels — the honeyed warmth of his deep, slow speech . . . she didn't understand how she could ever have listened to him before and not noticed how he sounded. His words, though heaven knew what they were, sounded like tender, intimate things spoken late at night; made her think of cool linen and warm, loving caresses.

Connor looked worried and waved his hands in front of her face. 'Are you OK, Jane?'

She dragged herself back to earth. 'I'm really, really fine . . . ' Feeling dazed, she forced herself to try to think clearly. The nearness of him was affecting her more and more right now. It was a very odd sensation, and it unnerved her. And clearly Connor was starting to notice. She excused herself hurriedly, muttering that she'd forgotten to do something, and got out of the kitchen as quickly as she could.

By the time she got back to the office, away from his presence, she was ashamed of her behaviour over the last half hour, and only too aware of the difficulties that might ensue if she carried on treating Connor like this. She walked up and down, unable to keep still. What was she to do? It was only yesterday she'd been talking to Fiona about relationships in the workplace, and how unpleasant it had been in one office when a manager had suddenly developed a (thankfully short-lived) crush on her.

She went to the window and, looking out at the windswept clouds, forced herself to listen to the voice of reason. *Look, this is a perfectly natural reaction to him. Every other woman he comes across feels the same way! But they can talk about it. You can't, and you mustn't show it — you're working together.*

She smiled wryly. What was it she'd said to Fiona? Mr White should have had more self-control, more respect for her as a work colleague. He might not have been able to control his *feelings*, while they lasted, but he should have controlled his *behaviour*. Well, she would just have to do the same.

It was time to get back to that lunch. Turning from the window, Jane smiled wryly to herself. It was probably just that Scottish villagers weren't accustomed to exotic men. If she lived in Los Angeles, say, handsome American males stripping off their shirts would be ten a penny. *I'll get used to him soon enough, and won't notice anymore.*

Ron had arrived by the time Jane got back to the kitchen, and she was pleased to find that at least in the meeting that followed she was able to behave perfectly normally. Connor had to leave after lunch to go to London; she went with Ron to find the contractors working on the pond, and stayed with them for the rest of the afternoon. She only returned to the cottage in time to have a bath and wash her hair before supper.

Fiona ran in from the studio as soon as her cousin arrived back at the cottage. She was bubbling over with wonderful news. She had heard from the ICA in London. It wanted to feature her work in an exhibition at their new site in Piccadilly, and she was ecstatic. Her face animated and eager, she could hardly get her tumbled sentences out fast enough. It was the really big step, the break she had been hoping for. She had already rung David; he was stopping off for champagne on his way home.

Jane was truly delighted for her. It was something they'd often discussed, but she'd heard Fiona dismiss it as a hundred-to-one shot so often, she'd assumed there was no realistic chance of it ever happening.

'You won't tell anyone else yet, will you?' said Fiona suddenly as they were all washing up the dishes companionably before taking their coffee into the garden. 'Sorry, that's a silly question. I know you wouldn't; it's just all so exciting.'

Jane hugged her cousin affectionately, dropping her tea towel in the process. 'Of course not. You've always kept all my secrets, haven't you?'

David picked up the tea towel and put it back on the side before carrying out the coffee into the garden. As they sat down together, he looked at them seriously. 'Talking of secrets, I found out something else from Robin — you know, my journalist friend — today. It's rather a sad story, I'm afraid, about Connor.'

Looking at Jane, he realised that although she had said nothing, she was all at once leaning towards him, her eyes fixed on him with an expression of painful anxiety. Her knuckles were white, tightened on her mug. He hesitated, but Fiona signalled to him — the smallest shake of her head — and he went on, picking his words carefully.

'He majored in anthropology at Harvard, and then did an MBA there. Before he started working for the Macaulay collection, he was employed by Cornell University on a project in Peru.'

As he was speaking, Jane visibly relaxed and interrupted him. Whatever she had been thinking of, it clearly wasn't this. 'Oh, that explains why he's got a picture of himself with a little South American family on his desk.'

David looked extremely uncomfortable. 'Well, actually that's probably . . . er, well . . . '

Fiona looked at him sharply. David cleared his throat and tried again. 'Connor's a widower. He was married to a colleague on the Cornell project, but she and her brother, and their daughter, died in a car crash in Peru about five years ago.' He cleared his throat again. 'So that's probably their photo.'

A silence fell. Jane felt quite numb for a moment. Then she felt tears prickling the back of her eyes as she experienced a wave of sorrow and sympathy for Connor. He had lost his beautiful wife and little girl.

She thought of their faces in the photograph, all so happy, laughing, hugging. Now his wife and child were gone. He was alone. A vivid picture sprang up of the afternoon they had spent cooking with Freya, while the little girl, who was normally so shy with strangers, chatted and confided, Connor listening attentively.

She looked across at the other two. Fiona had put her head in her hands on first hearing the news; now she straightened up, and Jane saw the glitter of unshed tears in her eyes, mirroring her own. 'Oh, David, what a terrible thing. Oh, poor Connor. And he's never told us!'

Suddenly Jane found herself trembling with anger, furious at these kind, well-meaning people who had no idea.

'Well, the problem is that once people know you're bereaved they can't forget it, and they treat you differently. They feel sorry for you and try not to disagree with you, so you never know whether they really like you or not. Like when I first came to live with you, Fiona — your mother and father always took my side when we argued, and I'd catch you all looking sorry for me.'

Fiona looked devastated. She reached out her hand over the table towards Jane. 'Oh Jane, I don't know what to say.'

Jane was immediately ashamed of her outburst. She took her cousin's hand in hers and squeezed it gently. 'It's all right. You all stopped doing that very quickly. But I do understand why Connor hasn't said anything. I haven't told him about my parents. You know, even though it happened during the war, it still has that sort of effect on people, and I didn't want him pigeon-holing me as an orphan and feeling sorry for me.' She paused. 'He hasn't exactly hidden it away, anyway. That photo of them together on his desk — it's always been there . . . ' She trailed off, feeling ashamed. Because they looked like local Peruvians, she hadn't even suspected that they might have been his family. She hadn't even thought to mention the photograph that stood on his desk every day.

And late that night, sitting at the window and looking out at the garden, Jane had to admit to herself that this news did make her feel differently about him. For over a month now, working with him, she had known Connor wasn't just a rich businessman. True, he was as hard as steel at his core, uncompromising on the things that really mattered to him. But he was much more than that. This warm, funny, modest, gentle man loved life so much.

She wasn't at all surprised about what he had done before shouldering the responsibilities of his inheritance. His grandfather would have been proud of him. It was difficult to think about it; thoughts jumbled and shifted. The only clear idea she had was a bright image of his wife and little girl looking out from the photograph, holding hands, so happy and confident.

Although Jane went to bed early, it

took her a long time to get to sleep that night. Her last thought as she drifted off was that Connor must have loved them very much.

7

David had to go to London early the next morning, and Fiona was going with him as far as Leuchars to see him off before shopping in St Andrews. They were very quiet getting up, but Jane was still woken by the six o'clock alarm, and once they were out of the house got up herself.

It was Tuesday; the specialist nursery she was using had arranged to send one of their horticulturists to visit that afternoon, the only date he could make in the next month or so. Meanwhile, she had the morning to spare, and wanted to use it to get a rough idea of what needed to be done to the boundaries of the estate, which were to be completely restored. Originally it had all been walled, but now much was in disrepair, and parts of the wall were fairly fragile, if not actually fallen down.

Whistling to Pip, and armed with her small camera and her notebook, Jane quietly let herself through the wicket gate and started to make her way along the boundary. Pip had already trotted ahead. The Shaws estate still seemed to have a particular fascination for him, perhaps because for so long he had not been allowed to go in.

The work called for all her concentration, and the effort and noise of breaking her way through what was virtually a young forest of self-sown trees and shrubs meant she couldn't hear Pip as she usually did when he was out of sight. But she assumed he would be near. He wouldn't go very far or very fast; he was too old for that.

It was a good twenty minutes later, stopping and calling before crossing a stream hidden in nettles, that she first became aware that Pip wasn't close to her. As her calls died away, a peculiar silence fell, broken only by some chaffinches calling from a beech nearby.

Then she heard distant, weak, whimpering. It sounded as if it was coming from further along the wall.

As she fought her way through brambles and bushes, Jane could start to hear the whimpering more clearly. Then she found him, trapped under broken concrete, barbed wire, and a rusty metal fence stake. He had probably been digging at a rabbit burrow, disturbed the fragile remains of the wall at this point, and it had fallen onto him.

She ran to him, slipping and sliding in her haste. He looked at her, whining, and she stroked his fur and murmured to him while trying to assess the extent of the damage. A large slab of concrete with the metal fence stake sticking up from it was pinning both back legs down.

She moved it with some effort and pushed it to one side for a moment, but it was far too heavy to lift away. Worse still, as she did so blood welled up, and she saw that one leg was not only crushed and useless, but also further trapped between a mess of barbed wire and stones. It would take much longer to manage to free him, and it was clear that it would need at least two people.

She thought fast. She needed to get to a telephone so that she could call the vet. If Dan advised her to bring Pip to the surgery, she would need someone to help her free him, but Fiona would not be back until lunchtime. Shaws was the nearest house, far closer than home. It had a telephone in the hall, and Connor would probably be there at this time in the morning. If not, she had a key to get in.

Meanwhile, making Pip as warm and comfortable as possible would help combat shock, and was worth the few moments of delay. Then she would have to leave him. She folded her sweater and put it under his head, and covered him with her coat; then, stroking his furry head, she told him to lie still, and that she would be back soon.

Her concern that Connor might be out was put to rest as she ran up to

Shaws; he opened the door as she got to it.

'I saw you running up the drive, Jane. Are you OK? You've hurt your ankle again, haven't you?'

She was too breathless to answer him in more than a few words. 'Foot's all right, just aches when I run. Pip's trapped — I can't get him out. Leg looks as if it's crushed. Can I ring the vet?'

He looked at her with concern, and moved out of the way quickly so that she could get to the phone behind him. 'What can I do?'

She had thought it all out, and spoke quickly and urgently to him as she dialled the number. 'Could you get a couple of blankets and towels, and something to lever the concrete block off him, and the first-aid kit from the kitchen? And could you go back with me?'

He was already halfway up the stairs, and called back over his shoulder, 'Yep — and I can get everything in two minutes. But what about your ankle?

Can you use it OK?'

'It's not a problem; I can manage it.' Jane's hand was shaking as she held the telephone receiver. She prayed that Dan had not yet gone out on calls, and drew a sharp breath of thanks as he answered in person.

Dan was extremely good in crises. He had instructed Jane about what to do by the time Connor returned, so she was able to share the information as they hurried back to Pip. 'He should be with us within the hour. We're to get the big slab of concrete off him, and try to stop any bleeding, but not to move him, just try to keep him still and warm and talk so he stays awake.'

By the time she had finished explaining, they were with Pip. To their immense relief, the blood flow was easily dealt with once the concrete slab was levered away, and they had even been able to gently move the stones trapping Pip's back legs and paws so that he could easily be moved once Dan had arrived. In a few minutes the main work was finished. There was nothing more now but be with Pip and wait.

They dropped onto their knees beside him and stroked his shaggy head and side. Pip looked up at them and raised a paw to Jane's knee, whining quietly. Jane patted it. 'You'll be more comfortable soon, darling, I promise.' She was quiet for a moment, stroking the dog gently.

Connor had risen and was standing slightly behind them, looking at them together, huddled on the ground. His heart went out to Jane, who had become very still. He sat down beside her, gently putting his hand on her shoulder for a moment. She turned and smiled at him briefly, and the stillness was broken.

In the end they had to stay with Pip for just over an hour, both quietly stroking him, trying to comfort him, Jane at his head, Connor at his side. The old dog looked at them, trying to move his head, and managing to wag his tail from time to time with a tired thump that sounded loud among the trees. There was no wind. Sunlight played on Pip's fur, showing up the matted blood and dirt. Then his eyes started to flutter and close, and all their efforts could not wake him. His breathing became more regular, but also more shallow.

'I can hardly see his ribcage moving,' said Jane worriedly. She took a deep breath and tried to control the catch in her throat. 'I think we might have to accept that he's going.'

Connor carefully lifted Pip's muzzle and spoke to him quietly but forcefully. 'Pip. Wake up, now. Wake up. Dan will be here in a moment, and you'll be just fine. Wake up.' He waited a few moments, then laid his head down again gently, but kept on stroking his side. 'He could be just sleeping. If he is, at least he isn't in any pain for a while.'

Jane looked at Connor, and their eyes met. 'Maybe.' She turned back, and he watched her, feeling helpless, as she bent down and hugged Pip, laying her cheek against the flap of his warm, furry ear. At that moment she looked very young and defenceless, and he could hardly hear her words. 'Don't go, Pip. Please don't go. I'm not ready for you to go yet, darling. Please come back to me.' But there was no response.

After a few moments she straightened up, searching blindly for a tissue, and was more grateful than she could say when Connor wordlessly offered her one. 'I'm so sorry. I'm overreacting.' She blew her nose and tried to compose herself.

'He means a lot to you,' said Connor. As he spoke, he realised that the words were awkward and wrong, but Jane didn't seem to notice. She twisted the tissue in her hands, put it in her pocket, and stroked Pip again. 'There, old fellow.' She paused. 'I guess it's because he's all I've got left from my mum and dad. They gave him to me for my tenth birthday, and they . . . ' This time her voice did break. ' . . . they passed away just after that.' She fished out the tissue and blew her nose again. 'There was an air raid. My dad was at home on leave. I know it all happened a long time ago, but . . . '

They were both quiet for a moment, and then Connor spoke. 'I don't think it matters how long ago it happened. And it's not overreacting.' He had not stopped stroking Pip, but his hand faltered as he said hesitantly, 'You may know already, though I haven't said to you — it's not a secret, but it's hard to talk about . . . I had a little girl and a wife. They died, five years ago in Peru. It's their photo on my desk.'

'I'm so sorry, Connor,' Jane said quietly. There was a pause, and she desperately searched for something to say. 'What was your wife's name?'

Connor swallowed hard and went on, his words starting to flow more easily. 'Laura. We grew up in the same neighbourhood, though she was away quite a lot because her parents were anthropologists and the whole family went on long field trips.'

Jane wanted to reach out and touch

him, but knew she must not. She kept stroking Pip, searching desperately for the right words. 'Did you spend much time in Peru?'

Connor smiled. 'Well, Laura and I had a dream that we'd both study anthropology, and then get MBAs from Harvard, so we could put business know-how to work in developing local communities. I guess philanthropy runs in my family; but I was pretty fed up with how it had turned out for my dad, spending every hour in meetings and worrying about insurance on paintings. I wanted to get out and work with people — like the scheme you're running with your garden — and so did she.' He paused, and then went on. 'Well, that's what we did. The day after we graduated we got married, and pretty soon after that we were working in South America, and Katie was born.' He swallowed hard. 'They died in a car crash three years later, with Brad, one of Laura's brothers.'

'He's in the photo too?'

Connor nodded. 'The photo was taken the day before the accident. He'd come over to visit from Boston, and they were going to spend a day up in the mountains.' He shook his head. 'It was pure chance I wasn't with them. One of our staff was ill, and I stayed behind to take him to the hospital.'

He stopped speaking for a moment, and his eyes looked into the distance. 'I got through their funeral pretty well. I had to. The whole family was . . . well, we were all in shock, and there were so many things to arrange.'

He stopped stroking Pip for a moment, and then went on. 'Well, I carried on living in the same house after the funeral, and went back to work almost straight away. I thought it was what she would have wanted, and it kept me from thinking too much.' He sighed. 'I was looking after all Katie's pets. She'd rescued a baby monkey, a little tamarin, from some boys that had gotten hold of it, and she loved it to bits. Well, that baby was a holy terror. She made messes all over the house, and broke into the food cupboard and was sick from all the candy, and screamed when she didn't get her own way. And we had to stay up all night to feed her every two hours at first, and she gave us all fleas. But she and Katie were so dam cute together. They always had baths with her holding on to Katie. She'd put her little arms round her neck, and hug her and look so angelic.'

He patted Pip. 'They would both have loved you, ol' feller, but that monkey would've driven you crazy.' He was silent for a moment, and looked at Jane. 'And afterwards she moped, and curled up in my arms — she'd never really bothered with me before — and all the spirit was gone out of her, for a long time.'

'She missed Katie too,' said Jane quietly.

Connor nodded. 'Well, I thought of that baby monkey when you were upset just now. After Laura and Katie died, I felt numb. And if I wasn't feeling numb, I was angry. I wasn't too easy to work with. But when that monkey died I cried like a baby. A snake bit her, and there was nothing I could do. I didn't cry at my family's funeral; but on my own, in my house, with Katie's pet — well . . . '

Jane nodded. 'It's as if they carry some of their love with them,' she said, and thought how clumsy her sentence was. But Connor understood her.

'Yes, I felt as if I was still caring for Katie when I looked after that little thing — being a loving parent, same as Laura and I had set out to be.'

Jane could only look at their hands, still stroking Pip, hers small and scratched; his large, capable, tanned. 'You understand,' she said.

She heard him give a quick, sharp intake of breath. 'I've only talked about this to one person before. Have you? Did they understand?'

She shook her head. 'No.' They were speaking rapidly and urgently now. In the distance they could just hear Dan calling.

'I better go get him,' said Connor. 'Here, let me help you up.' He got up quickly and held his hand out to her. Jane put her hand in his, and as she stood up they drew back for a moment, looking at each other, and briefly hugged each other. She was overwhelmingly aware of warmth and strong arms around her. Connor's rough warm cheek brushed against hers, and he had gone.

Then the moment of waiting passed, so quickly that she wondered afterwards whether it had been a dream. The next few minutes were a blur of intense activity, instructions and directions, as Dan arrived and took charge; and then she was limping back to the cottage, alone.

★　★　★

Fiona arrived back from St Andrews at lunchtime to find Jane huddled on the sofa beside the telephone, an odd blank look on her face. 'What on earth's the matter?' she asked worriedly.

Jane looked up, still hugging her

164

knees. 'It's Pip. He's been hurt. Dan and Connor took him to the surgery. I'm waiting to hear.' She jumped up suddenly, unable to sit still a moment longer, pent-up nervousness breaking out at last. 'Fiona, I'm so worried! They went nearly two hours ago, and I haven't heard from Connor yet. Anything could have happened. I'm worried that he hasn't phoned by now. Do you think he's all right?'

Fiona took her by the shoulders and shook her gently. 'Jane, why haven't you rung him or Dan?'

Jane looked up, an arrested look in her eyes. 'D'you know, I hadn't thought of that.' She hugged Fiona briefly. 'Oh, Fiona, I feel such a fool. Everything has gone wrong and I don't know what to do. I can't ring up. It'll look as if I don't trust them. I'm sure they'll ring as soon as there's any news. I don't want to chivvy them when they've probably got some good reason not to have called yet. I just wish I knew what's been happening . . . ' Her voice trailed away.

Fiona got up and went away for a few moments. She came back from the kitchen with a tray and handed a small glass of whisky to Jane. 'Here, drink this,' she said firmly.

Jane shook her head. 'You know I don't drink that stuff,' she said with something of her usual spirit.

'For goodness' sake,' said Fiona, losing patience, 'get it down you and stop messing about!'

Jane took a sip, coughed, spluttered, and sneezed as the fiery liquid caught the back of her throat.

'Now, drink this,' said Fiona inexorably, giving her a mug of tea.

If anything, the tea tasted even worse. 'You know I hate sugar in tea, too,' grumbled Jane; but Fiona, looking at her closely, noticed the colour starting to come back to her face as the liquids had their effect.

She sat down beside her, and when Jane seemed a little calmer, said gently, 'I think one of us ought to ring the vet, Jane. At least we'll get a little more information about what's going on.'

Jane nodded wordlessly. She felt too wretched to speak, but pulled herself together enough to give a brief outline of what had happened.

'He insisted on going because he noticed I was limping after I ran to Shaws for help. Anyway, someone had to stay behind to see to the landscapers, who didn't turn up for ages . . . and the horticulturalist is coming this afternoon — I ought to go and check on them again, actually . . . '

'All right, you do that,' said Fiona briskly. 'And meanwhile, I'll see if I can contact Dan, and I'll make some lunch. You may not feel like eating,' she added, catching Jane's protest before she'd started to speak, 'but I do.'

The walk over to where the landscapers were working, which took rather longer than usual with her stiff and sore ankle, helped to clear Jane's head. She felt ashamed of herself. Since getting back home and binding up her foot, she'd meant to get on with her own work, but had been unable to do a thing, and had been sitting by the phone imagining the worst. Going back to the office, finding the paperwork, talking to the foreman and dealing with timesheets, she was able to put everything into some perspective. Nevertheless, she hurried back home once the work was done, hoping to find that Fiona had good news. Her heart beat fast as she walked as quickly as she could up the path.

Fiona came out of the cottage as she neared the kitchen door. 'Everything's OK, Jane. I rang Dan and spoke to him and to Connor. They'd only just finished treating Pip, and Connor stayed with him the whole time — that's why you didn't get a phone call.'

Jane felt sick with relief. But she still had to make sure. 'So he's really going to be all right? What about internal bleeding?'

Fiona shot a quick glance at her. She was still very white. 'Honestly, it's all fine. Come and sit down. Here, have some coffee. Lunch in half an hour.'

Jane took the coffee gratefully. She hadn't bothered to put a jacket on and it had been drizzling with rain all morning. Her hair and clothes were still misted with water, and the warmth of the mug made her realise how cold her hands were.

'Connor said he'd be back soon. Dan wants to keep Pip for a couple of days to monitor how he does, so he won't be bringing him back today. But he's going to stay until Pip comes round from the anaesthetic, and see how he is before he sets off.'

Jane smiled for the first time since the accident. 'That's really kind of him.' Sipping the coffee, she slowly started to feel warmer, and thought about what had happened with Connor while they had been waiting for the vet to arrive. She looked up to see Fiona curled up on the sofa, regarding her quizzically.

'Away with the fairies for a moment there?' she enquired, raising one eyebrow. 'I wouldn't worry — he's a very sensible chap.'

Jane blushed; she couldn't help it. 'How did you know I was thinking about Connor?'

Fiona laughed outright. 'You should see the look on your face whenever you do — it's a picture. Come on, let's have some lunch. You'll feel much better once you've had something to eat . . . Bless me, who's that at the door?'

Jane had hardly had time to think, stupidly, that perhaps it was Connor, and then that of course it couldn't be — he was an hour's drive away — before there was a confused murmur of voices at the door.

'Daisy Redfern?' came Fiona's voice. 'Yes, of course I remember. London, wasn't it? . . . No, not at all . . . Please do come in, and meet my cousin Jane.'

Within moments she was back in the room with perhaps the most beautiful woman Jane had ever seen in her life. Tall, lissom, with wide grey eyes set in a flawless face. Clothes that even Jane, with her incurable hopelessness with fashion, recognised as perfectly chosen.

Golden hair that seemed to swing and gleam with effortless grace. The apparition seemed to fill the small room with her presence, and made even Fiona, up to now Jane's touchstone of elegance, look a little drab and grey.

Jane had sprung up from the sofa on hearing Fiona's invitation, cursing inwardly, as always, Fiona's hospitality. She'd never regretted this trait in her cousin as much as she did right now. She was feeling crumpled and frumpy as it was, and certainly didn't feel at all hospitable herself. And on seeing the visitor, her heart sank right down to her very serviceable socks. She fought down an overwhelming desire to look down at them and check whether the hole in the right heel showed.

But she had no more time to think; the vision swept forward, smiled (showing perfect white teeth) and held out her hands. Jane took them and found herself being embraced warmly by the beautiful stranger, who, having air-kissed her on both rather grubby cheeks, stood back and looked her up and down, all the while smiling and talking delightedly.

'My, I am so pleased to meet you. Connor's told me so much about you that I just couldn't bear it — I had to come along and see for myself!'

'It's lovely to meet you too,' said Jane, wondering furiously who she could possibly be.

The vision stopped suddenly and stepped back, turning to look earnestly at them both. 'You don't tell me — now wouldn't that be just like him? Connor hasn't said anything about me at all, has he?'

Fiona exchanged glances swiftly with Jane, and was just about to say something when their visitor interrupted.

'I can tell. You poor things, having me arrive like this! I should introduce myself properly. I'm here because I'm one of Connor's oldest friends. We met at college, and we kept in touch ever since because he was interested in my work. And well, let's just say we've been best buddies, especially after Laura died. He was inconsolable, and so was I. We talked for hours . . . We were all best friends at college, and Katie was my goddaughter. And ever since the summer and his disappearing off the scene, and telling all his staff not to bother him, meanwhile I was getting all these phone calls and emails about what a wonderful place his grandpa's old house was, and all about you all!

'Of course, he's told me all about how very kind you've been to him, especially since he's never been to Scotland before except for that one visit, and thought you might not be too pleased to see him again, wondering why he was buying up the old house. I'm so glad it's all working out so well . . . but I just couldn't bear not seeing him any longer! Well, right now there's some administrative problem in London with my partnership — don't ask me, my math is stuck in first grade — and it's holding everything up right now. Kim had to come over to deal with it, so I thought I might as well come over here too, and surprise Connor. But he doesn't seem to be at the house — what a truly wonderful old house that is; I'm not surprised he's fallen in love with it — so I thought I'd try here, and it's just swell to find you at home!'

She paused for breath, and smiled at them. 'D'you know where my darling boy is? I'm truly dying to see him!'

8

As she listened to this slightly breathless introduction, Jane straightened herself, mentally shook herself up, and at the first sign that their visitor was drawing breath, heard herself joining Fiona in asking Daisy to stay for lunch.

It was impossible not to like her. It was also clear from her conversation with Fiona that they were already acquainted. Daisy was well known in the art world, working on casts and sculptures; and even Jane had heard of her collaboration this year with the Australian artist Blake Ross.

Yes, it was impossible not to like Daisy — she was so open, so engaging, so unfeignedly friendly and interested. She was sincerely horrified when Jane explained why Connor wasn't at home, and immediately offered to leave, relenting only when they protested that her visit would take their minds off Pip's accident.

But Jane, looking at her, smiled wryly to herself. Ever since Daisy had walked through the door, she had been forced to admit that all her hopes about Connor, all her feelings for him — which she had only just acknowledged to herself — were probably dashed by this smiling, lovely stranger. It was very clear indeed how close Daisy was to Connor. She must surely be the 'other person' that he had mentioned just a couple of hours ago. The times Jane had thought he'd been interested in her as more than a working colleague . . . well, she must just have misinterpreted his actions. After all, he was such a charismatic man.

What had happened between them this morning was a perfect example. He was so kind, so sympathetic. It was just as well Daisy had turned up, or Jane realised she might have read too much into what had happened.

Her train of thought was broken as Fiona came through from the kitchen to say that lunch was ready. Daisy jumped up. 'My, I must go freshen up. May I use your bathroom?'

Jane smiled at her. 'Of course — it's just up the stairs. Come into the kitchen when you're done.'

Going through to the kitchen herself with Fiona, and crossing over to the stone sink to wash her hands, Jane sighed. She knew that her cousin would never dream of discussing a guest in the house. Barred from gossip, politeness would have to do, though she was dying to know if Fiona knew anything more about Daisy.

'Thank you for making lunch,' she said, turning to the covered dishes on the cooking range. 'Let me help you carry this lot over.'

'No, not at all — you've had quite enough to deal with for one day.'

Fiona was clearly in big-cousin mode, and Jane was about to argue; but the doorbell rang, and Fiona was distracted. 'Do rest your foot, Jane — well, all right then, thank you. That'll be Bruce and Aileen back from church. I'll just go and say we're about to eat.'

Jane hobbled over with two of the salads. Her foot had really stiffened up, but she was determined not to let that stop her from doing yet more things. Putting the dishes carefully down on the table, her back to the window, the midday sun streaming in behind her, she was perfectly placed to see Connor coming in one side of the kitchen with Fiona, as Daisy came in the other.

They both stopped for a split second. Then it was as if time had started again, and Jane watched with an indescribable sensation in her stomach as they ran to each other and Connor enveloped Daisy in an enormous bear hug.

Daisy was a tall woman, but she was lifted her off her perfectly shod feet, and Jane caught a glimpse of their heads together, his dark hair against her gold. Then they were standing back, holding hands, laughing, Daisy immediately talking nineteen to the dozen.

'Darling Connor, I just couldn't bear not seeing you any longer. Blake had to come over to London to sort out this horrible mess over the imports, so we had to stop work anyway. I tried your house — I must tell you what a truly amazing house that is! — and you weren't in, so I came over here.' She threw out her hands gracefully to include the others. 'And you both have been so kind, inviting me to lunch, and especially with poor darling Pip.' She turned back to Connor. 'I was saying to them that I couldn't wait to see them after all you've told me!'

Connor smiled back at her. 'Daisy, I sure am glad to see you too.' He turned to Jane and Fiona. 'Daisy is just about my oldest friend — we met in our first week at college.'

As he spoke, Jane was struck again by what a beautiful couple they made — both so tall, he so handsome, she so exquisitely made up, and perfectly dressed. Connor had clearly gone home before coming over to the cottage. He was no longer wearing the jeans he'd had on that morning, but dark trousers and a white linen shirt, very like what he'd had on when he'd first turned up at the cottage that summer. Then, Jane had been so angry with him, so sure he was about to destroy the spirit of Shaws and spoil one of the landmarks of the village. Now she knew him so much better, and she wasn't angry with him anymore — no, not at all, never. She sighed, and mentally set herself to make conversation with the happy couple.

But Connor, after drawing out a chair for Daisy, walked to the other side and sat down next to Jane. 'I did leave Pip absolutely fine, you know. Dan Campbell said we can go over to see him tomorrow.' He was looking at her, a slight crease between his brows. As she looked back at him, she saw his forehead clear, and he smiled. 'So it's all over, and all fine.' He leant over to Daisy. 'You arrived at the end of some crisis, hon.' He turned back to Jane. 'He'd woken up before I left, though he's still pretty woozy. But Dan says we might even be able to bring him back tomorrow.'

The last nagging feelings of doubt and worry about Pip ebbed away, and Daisy and Fiona, watching closely, saw Connor and Jane grinning at each other delightedly, like two children at the beginning of the holidays.

'Why, that's marvellous!' cried Daisy. 'Darlings, you must be so happy!'

Jane could only nod. Ridiculously, she felt a catch in her throat, and had to fish out her handkerchief and blow her nose hard.

'Will you be able to stay for long in Crail?' Fiona asked Daisy as they started to help themselves to the salads and Jane poured water for everyone.

Daisy turned to her, smiling. 'Well, heaven knows Blake's a marvel at unravelling bureaucracy, but even he thinks it might be a day or two before this particular problem gets sorted out. So we'll definitely be in Edinburgh for the beginning of the week at least, and I'm hoping I can get him to come over and visit here too.' She leaned over to Jane. 'You'd love him, I know, and he's dying to meet you all too.' She turned to Connor. 'Tell them now, isn't he adorable? You thought so straight away, didn't you?'

Connor smiled at her. 'Well, I only met him a couple of times before the wedding, you know; but now I come to think of it, yes, perhaps I should have mentioned I was rather attracted to him myself . . . I did try to warn you, but . . .'

Daisy exploded into laughter. 'Quit bugging me!' She turned to Jane and Fiona. 'You know, Blake and I got together so quickly I can still hardly believe it's happened. I hadn't even met him this time last year, but I hoped he'd agree to work on an installation with me because I admired his work so much. So I travelled out to Australia to meet him in the spring, and well . . . it was incredible. He came over to work in Boston as soon as he could. I knew right away, and so did he. Our parents were hoping for a long engagement and fancy wedding, but we just quietly went

182

right out and got married this summer at our local church!'

Jane's hand trembled so violently that she nearly dropped the water jug. 'You've just got *married* to Blake?' she said to Daisy, unable to keep the surprise out of her voice, and unable to stop another delighted smile from spreading across her face. She fought back an overwhelming desire to look back at Connor.

Daisy misunderstood her surprise. 'Yeah! I know all the papers said we were set for a long engagement, and *Vogue* did that ridiculous article about how we were waiting to see how well we could work together before the wedding. But it was all really because of our mothers wanting to arrange it all. In the end we just couldn't bear it, and the wedding was so quiet that it wasn't picked up by the press, especially because it was right in the week of the Super Bowl finals — so nobody really knows about it, which is just fine by us!'

★　★　★

After lunch, Connor and Fiona insisted on washing up, leaving Jane and Daisy with coffee and biscuits on the sofa in the living room. Jane protested, but they were adamant. As soon as they had gone through into the kitchen, Daisy put her coffee cup down and turned to her.

Jane was surprised to see a shade of anxiety in those beautiful eyes. She wondered what the matter could be, but almost immediately Daisy started to speak.

'Jane, I'm so glad I have the chance to talk to you on our own. I was quite sure I might not be able to, but I thought it was worth the journey, and Blake thought so too . . . And now I'm so glad, because you're so perfect together, and anyone can see that, but Connor — well, I thought I must try to do something, and I can.' She paused for breath.

'I don't quite understand,' said Jane carefully, though she could feel her heart starting to beat painfully quickly, and the colour rising in her face.

Daisy reached out to her impulsively. 'Jane, you must know that he's in love with you.' As Jane remained quite still, she went on, 'All his letters to us — his phone calls, to his family too . . . it's so clear, and it all hit him by surprise because he thought he would never be with anyone again after Laura died. But that was five years ago . . . And now he's thinking he hasn't got a chance, since he can't say anything because of your working together on the house, and being neighbours. And besides, he thinks you'd never be interested in him, because he acted so stupid the first time he ever met you.'

She paused, and a sad look crossed her expressive face. 'He still hadn't really gotten over Laura then, you know.' She shook her head briefly. 'And then when he came back to Scotland, it turned out you thought he'd insulted you by making an offer on your house! Oh, Jane. Is that still a problem?'

Jane realised that her expression must

have given her away. 'Well it is, because we rowed so badly about it, and haven't discussed it since. The trouble is, I feel quite differently about that now . . . quite differently. And I haven't told him so.' She sighed. 'It just never seems to be the right time, and I don't know what he would say.'

Daisy reached out her hand impulsively. 'Jane, you must tell him. Everything will turn out all right, you'll see.'

Jane smiled — Daisy's confidence was infectious — and her new friend smiled back at her.

'Darling Connor. We realised how crazy in love he was with you when he messed up so bad all the time. It's the first I ever knew of him having such spectacular failures! He's usually so diplomatic and tactful. It was then we all knew he was really serious about you.'

Jane stared at her. 'Did . . . did he tell you all of this?'

Daisy laughed. 'No, of course not. But it's obvious from what he's been saying about you, and it's not just me who thinks that. His mom thinks so too, and all his family, and Laura's family, and our friends. The only person who doesn't believe it is Juanita — she's Laura's aunt, and she's . . . well, she's getting a bit older now, and if you ask me she doesn't want to believe it, but it's only because she's always been a bit shy with strangers, and it's her turn to host Thanksgiving, and she says she hasn't got enough special plates for anyone else. I told her I'll make one for her if I have to!'

Jane felt bemused. She had never thought of Connor having any living relatives, but at a stroke Daisy had conjured up an invisible host of protective people standing around him on guard. She picked on the most extraordinary fact of this odd conversation. 'Connor still keeps in touch with Laura's family?'

Daisy laughed. 'They're his family, and they always will be. Laura's mom is his godmother. They still live in the same neighbourhood, and he has eight nephews and nieces who run rings around him. You never saw such a good uncle.' Her face clouded for a moment. 'He was a good dad, too.'

Jane nodded, glad to be able to say something. 'Yes, he must have been. I've never seen anything like the way he gets on with my own goddaughter, and she's normally so quiet with strangers.'

Daisy's exquisite brow suddenly furrowed. 'Connor still being close to Laura's family — you didn't know that before? Does it bother you?'

Jane laughed, and then looked at her soberly. She was touched by Daisy's concern. 'I think it's wonderful.'

Daisy clapped her hands together. 'I knew it! Darling, from the moment I saw you together I knew you were just so right for each other. I really hope it all works out for you both. It's just that we all thought he might be trying so hard to act respectful that you wouldn't even realise how he felt. He hasn't said anything, has he?'

Jane paused for a moment, trying to

collect her thoughts. Daisy had come a long way to talk to her, and to help her friend. She deserved an honest, considered response to what she had said.

'Well, no, he hasn't in so many words. There have been times when I wondered whether maybe . . . but I thought it was just me being unrealistic. I thought . . . But then there have been so many misunderstandings, so many times when I've been so angry with him — even at first . . . ' Her self-possession deserted her. They were bound to be interrupted any moment now, and the chance to talk would be lost.

Leaning towards Daisy, she said quickly, 'I'm sorry, I'm not putting this very clearly. I made mistakes, and said things wrong, and some things I wish I hadn't said, because I don't think them anymore.'

She took a deep breath. Somewhere, deep below her usual thoughts, a bubble of joy was starting to grow within her. 'He really does love me?'

It started out as a question, but

ended on a rising note of happiness as she and Daisy smiled at each other. There was no time to say more. Connor and Fiona were walking through from the kitchen.

★　★　★

The rest of the day passed in a blur. Connor arranged to take Daisy around the local sights that afternoon, and urged Fiona and Jane to join them. Fiona accepted, but Jane declined politely. Suddenly she was feeling very shy with Connor. And not only did the landscapers need to be watched pretty closely, but she really needed to keep the appointment with the salesman from the specialist tree nursery. And she needed to be alone, to think.

But by the time her work was finished, she realised that she had had no time for thinking about Connor at all. She was exhausted, and her foot was quite seriously painful, and her head was aching badly. Connor rang to invite her along to the restaurant to which they were going. He tried his best to persuade her, but Jane was adamant, and explained about her foot, and her headache.

But they were not the only reasons that she had. To be honest with herself, she was still feeling desperately shy. Privately, she thought that she could not think of anything worse right now than spending the evening with Connor and a newly married couple, however adorable they were. She needed time on her own, and was very glad indeed that Connor was going to be staying on in Edinburgh the next day as well.

Part of her could not still quite believe Daisy, but at the same time the realisation that it was true — that he did love her — was slowly taking hold. Thinking back over the times they had been together, the ways he had acted all started to fall into place, and how she had acted as well. And at last her own feelings, so confused for so long, were becoming crystal clear.

By the next day, Jane felt a great deal better. Over breakfast she talked cheerfully to Fiona about the evening before, though of course the question that she really wanted to know the answer to, but which was left unspoken, was: *'Did Connor miss me?'*

Just as they were finishing breakfast, the telephone rang. Jane jumped up to answer it and hastily looked at Fiona, who nodded understandingly and took herself off to the studio.

The phone call took a long time — Jane dashed over to ask her for a pencil and notepad at one point — and Fiona smiled to herself, assuming Connor had called. But when Jane came back into the studio, she was walking rather slowly. Fiona glanced at her, and then again, sharply. 'Is everything OK?'

Jane sat down in the rocking chair. 'Yes. No. I mean, yes. That was Christie's. I mean, it was the head of the modern art section at Christie's. You and David were right about those paintings, Fiona. Look, I wrote down the names of the artists.'

Fiona peered at the scrap of paper. 'Hmm. And is that the total valuation at the bottom?'

Jane nodded wordlessly.

Fiona dropped her tea towel and hugged her. 'Oh Jane!' She laughed. 'I thought it was a pretty good chance, but I can't quite believe it.'

Jane buried her head in her hands. 'I've got to talk to a lawyer about this. Today.'

Fiona squeezed her shoulder. 'I agree. And, Jane — don't talk to anyone else about this until then.'

Jane nodded again, and smiled for the first time. 'That's just what the man from Christie's said.'

9

By nine o'clock the next day, the time that she and Connor usually met up at Shaws, Jane was ready to go across. The builders wouldn't be in till twelve, but there was lots of paperwork to be done before then. Besides, Connor had promised to take her to see Pip. And perhaps, just perhaps, it might be possible for her to say the things she needed to say to him.

She squared her shoulders as she marched through her garden, feeling absurdly nervous, but on the other side of the wicket gate was brought up by surprise as she heard a door slam and saw Connor emerge from around the corner of the house and come running towards her. She saw he was wearing his ancient old jeans again today, with a college shirt that looked faded and worn. He was filthy with dust and cobwebs again, and his hair was rumpled wildly, but he was smiling at her. Did he have some good news?

'Honey, it's the most wonderful thing! You remember I was going through the packing cases? I found a notebook of my grandpa's about building the house. It goes through everything in the most amazing detail. He even sketched the designs of how he wanted each room.'

Laughing, he lifted her up and swung her round as easily as if she were a child. Jane hardly heard what he said, but his mood was infectious, and she started to laugh too, for the sheer joy of it. She remembered Daisy's words — *'He's in love with you'* — and completely forgot about all the serious things she had meant to say to him. As soon as he put her down, she flung her arms around him and hugged him. 'I'm so pleased . . . '

He swung her up again in the cool fresh air. 'Honestly, is this the way you usually celebrate good news?' she said, slightly breathlessly.

He grinned at her and put her down.

'Haven't you seen *any* American movies? We always do this, especially if we haven't seen someone for two days!'

'My taste runs more to British cinema,' said Jane primly and wholly untruthfully. 'Where everyone has a wee dram to celebrate. Of course, nowadays people are really more likely to air-kiss each other, twice on either cheek. It's the European way. Didn't you see the newsreel when Volare won Eurovision?'

He smiled down at her and raised a quizzical eyebrow. 'Seems I'm out of practice on European etiquette. Does it include hugging people too, like you just did?'

She laughed right back up at him. 'Of course it does, if one of you has just had really good news. And don't you kid me. You must spend half your time talking to French museum committees.'

'Mmm, but they'd all jumped on board the American management train by last fall, and now they all act as if they're being filmed for Hollywood.' He paused and smiled down at her.

196

'Perhaps you'd better show me how I gotta do it here, honey.'

She felt a rush of affection for the gentle, good-natured man beside her. Stretching up, she put her hands on his shoulders and, carefully placing her cheek next to his, kissed the air. 'There you are!'

'And now the other cheek? Like this?'

Without her quite realising how, or why, they did it, and did it again.

'Jane?' He looked down at her tenderly, in a way she'd never seen before. Her eyes fluttered shut and opened; his had darkened to a smoky black. His lips grazed her cheek. Timidly she reciprocated; then he was kissing the corner of her mouth, and she his.

Connor's hand came up from her shoulders to the back of her head, and he slowly stroked her hair down to the nape of her neck. She shivered with yearning. Stepping closer to him, she drew his head down against her cheek, his warm sweet breath on her face. She could feel the short, quick rise and fall of his chest against her. They could only hear each other breathing.

Slowly Jane drew away from him to look at his face, that familiar face of a friend that was no longer familiar, but held an unknown and irresistible magic. It was as if the world had turned upside down. Connor reached out to her, his eyes searching hers, cupped her face in his hand, and stroked her cheek. She felt quite dazed. The speed of events had taken her by surprise.

'I, er, I wasn't expecting this right now . . . ' she croaked, but reached up to stroke his hair.

Connor smiled at her very tenderly. He put one hand on her shoulder, the other on her waist, and gently, insistently, drew her to him again. She could feel the warmth of his body, the rough cloth of his shirt against her cheek, and he stroked her hair in return.

'It's not exactly what I was expecting, either, this morning.'

His voice shook, and Jane could hear his breathing quicken. His hands tightened, and her head was swimming. They were both shaking. Jane, quite unable to stop herself, turned her head so that together, in the space of a breath, their lips met.

She felt his mouth against hers, and then there was a sigh of mutual longing, and they kissed frantically. Jane could feel his body strong and warm against hers, his hands hungrily holding her warm taut skin, his fingers digging into her shoulders, her arms, her back. She was doing exactly the same thing, and she felt as if she would never be able to stop.

But it must have been only a few moments later that they were shocked apart as they heard a perfect fusillade of barking and yapping coming close. As Jane stepped back, a small black Scottish terrier ran and jumped up at her, while another dropped a small red ball at Connor's feet and barked expectantly, waiting for him to throw it for them. It was the minister's very badly behaved dogs, Hamish and Mactavish, and the minister himself was just coming into view.

Jane swallowed hard and tried to pull herself together. She felt quite dazed. Within a moment the minister was with them, and they were exchanging the usual polite courtesies. He was hoping that they would sponsor a new fundraising effort for the kirk.

He refused the offer of refreshments, but came into Shaws with them, and talked for a very long time. They both signed up without any demur at all, and the old man was delighted. Jane blinked at the amount Connor put his name down for.

'I'll be announcing the fund at the next service, my dears,' he said, beaming at them short-sightedly from behind his spectacles. 'But it's good of you, very good of you, to help start it up. It always makes a wee bit of difference when folk hear people have already contributed.'

At last he went, and they waved goodbye as he went down the path, the little dogs gambolling about him. Connor carefully closed the door and turned round. They both started laughing.

'Oh, I do hope he didn't notice anything!' gasped Jane, wiping her eyes.

Connor ran his hands through his hair so that it was even more rumpled than before. 'Let's have that coffee I made hours ago,' he said.

In the kitchen he poured them both the extremely strong black coffee he always had waiting when she arrived for work. As he did so, the metal pot rattled. She leaned against him, he put his arm around her, and she put her head against his shoulder.

They were very still; but just as she had felt in her own kitchen when Connor had first visited her in the cottage, Jane felt excessively wide awake. The nerve endings of her whole body seemed to be concentrated on his presence. Every sense was heightened.

Connor stroked her hair gently. Her longing for him was becoming overwhelming, and she could feel his hand shaking. She knew that in another moment they would be kissing again. Closing her eyes momentarily, she shook her head as if she was trying to get water out of her eyes, trying to dispel the fog, trying to remember what she had been thinking about since she last saw him.

'Really, truly, Connor, do you think this is a good idea? After all, you're my employer.'

Connor's eyes, so warm and bright a moment ago, clouded. Standing absolutely still, he looked down at her hand in his, and stroked it gently. 'But I think we've gotten to know each other pretty well, Jane. And people do get together at the office — you can't stop them. Prohibitions never work. Besides, you're only working for me for the summer.'

Jane sighed. 'We have got to talk, Connor. It's not just about us. I have some important things I need to tell you as well.'

To hide her confusion, she very deliberately took her hand away, dragged over two chairs and sat down on one, gesturing to the other. After a little hesitation, Connor sat on it, leaning towards her, elbows on his knees, his hands clasped so tight that his knuckles showed white, his eyes fixed on hers.

Jane sat up straight in her chair, hands clasped on her knees, painfully conscious of trying to find the right words to say. 'I've been doing a lot of thinking about my house over the last few weeks, Connor. You know, the cottage and Shaws feel like a part of me, because they hold so many memories. And when I first met you, I thought you were trying to take all that away from me, and change everything.'

She paused thoughtfully, and then smiled at him. 'But I don't feel that way anymore, Connor. I love the cottage and the garden, and Shaws, but so do you. Your plans keep everything just the way I'm happy with . . . the way my grandparents would've wanted.'

She leant forward and held out her hand to him. His hands started to play with hers, and she found that she was answering; their fingers were twining and intertwining as she spoke.

'I've been thinking about my plans

for the gardening business and the scheme I want to set up for disabled children. David and Fiona were quite right. Your offer did — does — make sense, because in the end, my property isn't terribly suitable for what I want to do.' She smiled wryly. 'The cottage and the garden are too big, and the studio . . . once Fiona and David find a place, I won't have any use for it. The Macaulay Foundation would be a much better owner. I don't want to take more than the market value. That isn't necessary, because — well, because Grandma left me some pictures. I got them valued recently. Here, I brought the list to show you.'

Connor took the paper. As soon as he glanced at the list he looked up at her, startled. 'Why, Jane — '

She broke in hurriedly. 'I'll need to sell one for capital, but I'll offer it to the Macaulay Foundation first. And if the trustees agree, it can have the rest on permanent loan.'

Connor looked at her with a curious

expression on his face. 'Darling, I don't know what to say. Do you realise just how much . . . Your offer isn't because . . . Sorry, that's a tomfool thing to say . . . Do you really mean it?'

Jane smiled at him and squeezed his hands back, hard. 'Yes, Connor. I do know exactly how much those paintings are worth. And my offer isn't out of some sense of duty, or because of us. That capital is all I need, and I'd like someone to appreciate those paintings your granddad collected — my grandparents didn't, and I certainly don't!' She smiled at him.

His voice was unsteady. 'You know, I don't think one person in ten thousand would've made that offer, Jane.'

She smiled at him lovingly. 'Well, I think you would, Connor. You know you would.'

He sighed and stroked her hand. 'Don't make me out to be something I'm not, darling. I've always had this sort of money. I don't know what I'd be like if I hadn't.' He paused. 'And once you've done all this, my darling, and the Macaulay Foundation owns your property, what then?'

Jane laughed. Suddenly she felt a great weight off her shoulders. She felt as light as air. 'Well, I'll have found another place nearby, much smaller, with a much more suitable garden for working with disabled children. There are a couple of places I've heard about that might be put on the market next spring, actually, and I'll take it from there. The business should work out just fine. I've had lots of requests for garden designs already, because of doing the work on Shaws. But the difference the capital will make is that I'll have the financial backing to be able to concentrate mainly on the children's scheme.'

She smiled at him. 'And what about you? What are you planning to do, once Shaws has been renovated and the project for the families is up and running?'

Connor looked at her seriously. His voice was low as he started to speak. 'I changed my mind about what I wanted to do after I got to know you, Jane. I've gone back to the sort of work I always wanted. You know, it was your example, your hopes and your plans, that helped me to do it.'

Jane was so embarrassed by this that for the life of her she could not raise her eyes to his, and mumbled something unintelligible.

Connor said gently, 'It was you that made me want to stay, Jane. And I can. The Foundation needs someone for its charity wing, so I can do the type of work I used to do for Cornell. And the trustees agreed I can do it for as long as I want to, based here.'

At this she looked at him, and he returned her gaze. A little silence fell. His eyes were black with longing, fixed on her face.

'I made so many mistakes at first, trying to get to know you. That's why, when you agreed to work for me, I decided to keep as professional as I could, just the way you asked. But I was hoping all along to get to know you better one day as a friend . . . and more. You know, honey, I think we could do everything we want in the future, but I'd like us to do it together. Say you feel the same way. Do you? Will you marry me?'

The silence stretched out. Jane was quite literally unable to speak for a moment; her heart was overflowing with affection and love. She reached out her hand to stroke his cheek.

'Oh, Connor. I don't know how to begin to tell you.'

Connor smiled back at her tenderly. 'Kiss me again, please?'

For an answer, she bent her head towards his. Their hands continued to twine. Still sitting on the separated chairs, they kissed gently, tentatively, and then again.

Epilogue

It was very still outside in the summer dawn, but Jane could hear the birds singing as she stretched out sleepily in the wildly rumpled bed. She turned over and looked at Connor, still sleeping beside her. Her heart turned over with a tug of affection. He looked absurdly innocent, considering the night before, with his dark eyelashes fanned onto his cheek.

She propped her head on her hand and leaned on one elbow, wondering whether to wake him or not. It was still half an hour before they had to get up. Then she heard the doorbell, but Connor still didn't stir. Sighing, she tugged on one of his old linen shirts, which came down to her knees, and trudged downstairs. The contractors were early again.

At the door, Jamie was apologetic,

but Jane smiled and assured him it didn't matter, especially today. As she turned to go back to bed, she heard a bedroom door open; going up the stairs, a hand stole into hers.

'Mummy, who was that?'

Jane lifted up her little son and kissed him, then turned back to go down to the kitchen, carrying him on her hip. 'That was Jamie, darling. He came early because the big tent is going up on the lawn today for everyone coming.'

Ted clapped his hands excitedly. 'Will Freya and James and Charlie be there? And Aunty Juanita, and all the grans and granddads, and all my big cousins — are they still here too?'

Jane laughed. 'Yes, of course they are, angel mine. And, remember, Aunty Fiona, and Uncle David, and all the little cousins, and Emma and baby Sam, and all the children who do gardening with us — they're coming over today too. And everybody'll be here for ages yet.' She opened the door into the kitchen. 'Look, here's Aunty Juanita, up already!'

'My, what a big boy, waking up so early for your big christening day,' said Aunty Juanita, resplendent in an enormous red and gold dressing gown. 'Come and give your *favourite* aunty a hug.'

Ted twisted out of Jane's arms like a shot and ran to her, climbing up onto her lap and putting his little arms around her. They both laughed uproariously at the joke, and Jane wagged her finger at them. 'Aunty, you'll get into trouble again when the other aunties hear you saying that!'

'Can I stay in the kitchen now, Mummy?'

'Yes, and you go on back to sleep, *cara mia*. You don't need to be up yet for a long time. Shall we make some cake for later, Teddy?' said Aunty Juanita.

Jane escaped and tiptoed back into her bedroom, locking the door. As she went towards the bed, Connor opened his eyes, and they both smiled.

We do hope that you have enjoyed reading this large print book.

Did you know that all of our titles are available for purchase?

We publish a wide range of high quality large print books including:
Romances, Mysteries, Classics
General Fiction
Non Fiction and Westerns

Special interest titles available in large print are:
The Little Oxford Dictionary
Music Book, Song Book
Hymn Book, Service Book

Also available from us courtesy of Oxford University Press:
Young Readers' Dictionary
(large print edition)
Young Readers' Thesaurus
(large print edition)

For further information or a free brochure, please contact us at:
Ulverscroft Large Print Books Ltd.,
The Green, Bradgate Road, Anstey,
Leicester, LE7 7FU, England.
Tel: (00 44) **0116 236 4325**
Fax: (00 44) **0116 234 0205**

Other titles in the
Linford Romance Library:

THE MOST WONDERFUL TIME OF THE YEAR

Wendy Kremer

After ditching her cheating boyfriend, Sara escapes to a small village for Christmas, expecting to find rest and relaxation without the usual seasonal stresses. But her landlady, Emma, soon involves her in the village's holiday preparations, and the magic of Christmas begins to weave its spell. While Sara settles in and makes new friends, she also relishes the special attentions of Emma's handsome neighbour, Alex, and his young daughter. Could she actually have a future here — and is this Christmas destined to be her best ever?

OFF LIMITS LOVER

Judy Jarvie

Practice nurse Anya Fraser's adopted son is the centre of her busy life. But once her village clinic's handsome new senior partner Dr. Max Calder arrives, he is suddenly in her thoughts more than she's ready to admit. When extreme sports fan Max volunteers to help her with a terrifying charity parachute jump, they grow close. But Anya soon learns that the leap of faith she must take will impact on the home life she's fought so hard to secure.

HUNGRY FOR LOVE

Margaret Mounsdon

When celebrity chef Charlie Irons is let go from his daytime cookery slot, Louise Drew becomes his replacement. But with minimal cookery experience, appalling on-air nerves and disastrous culinary experiments, she is unable to sustain viewing figures and is sacked. She applies for a new job as a personal assistant with catering experience, but realises to her horror that it would mean working for Charlie Irons — and looking after two headstrong young girls. Is Louise up to the task, especially when Charlie's glamorous ex-wife arrives on the scene?

THE MISTRESS OF ROSEHAVEN

Rosemary Sansum

Left widowed and in debt, Rosemary Shaw has no choice but to accept an invitation from an uncle she has never met to come and live at his Rhode Island mansion, Rosehaven. But from the minute she arrives with her young children, she finds the place ominous and unsettling. Even as she begins to fall in love with the mysterious Will Hennessy, it seems that someone is prepared to go to any lengths to prevent Rosemary from becoming the new mistress of Rosehaven . . .

PLAYING MUM

Sarah Purdue

Freya Hardy's sister Astrid has been called for jury service, so she offers to take care of her two nieces and nephew while putting her travelling plans on hold. But Freya soon discovers that being a stand-in mum is much harder than being an auntie . . . Jamie Barnes, deputy head at her nephew's school, is unimpressed with Freya's efforts, and the two of them clash — but when Jamie steps in to help during a crisis, their relationship changes. And when Astrid returns, Freya has a decision to make about her future . . .

NURSE ON SKIS

Phyllis Mallett

Kay is delighted to be back in Scotland. A new job — district nurse — is waiting, and her boss is her uncle, Dr. Edgar Duncan, a GP in Stranduthie. Excited about her new life and the challenge of covering three villages in a remote area, she quickly settles into a routine. Dr. Clive Farrell, her uncle's new partner in the practice, soon falls for her, and she feels attracted to him as well. The path of true love runs smoothly until Dr. Frank Munro arrives, seemingly intent on ruining Kay's dream . . .